Flight and Other Stories

Western Literature Series

FLIGHT
and Other Stories

JOSÉ SKINNER

University of Nevada Press ▲▲ Reno & Las Vegas

Western Literature Series

University of Nevada Press, Reno,

Nevada 89557

Copyright © 1994, 1995, 1996, 1998, 2000,

2001 by José Skinner

Manufactured in the United States

of America

Library of Congress Cataloging-in-

Publication Data

Skinner, José, 1956–

Flight and other stories / José Skinner.

p. cm. — (Western literature series)

ISBN 0-87417-359-0 (alk. paper)

1. Hispanic Americans — Fiction.

I. Title. II. Series.

PS3569.K499 F57 2001

813'.6 — dc21   00-011122

10 09 08 07 06 05 04 03 02 01

5 4 3 2

For Babs

Contents

Acknowledgments

The author acknowledges the original publishers of the following stories: "Age of Copper" in *Witness* (2001); "Cosas, Inc." and "Archangela's Place" in *Blue Mesa Review* (1995, 1996); "Careful" in *Boulevard* (2000); "Dogs" in *Frontera Literary Review* (1998); "Eloy" (as "Families") in *Revista Bilingüe/Bilingual Review,* Arizona State University, Tempe, vol. 20, no. 1 (January–April 1995); "Spring" and "Flight" in *Saguaro* (1994, 1996); "Pickup" in *descant* (1995); and "Weeds" in *Western Humanities Review* (1998).

And the author gives a special and heartfelt thanks to Doug Unger, Trudy McMurrin, and Alberto Ríos for their invaluable help in bringing this collection to light.

Flight and Other Stories

Flight

On an overcast November afternoon, a Taos County sheriff's deputy drove up the deeply rutted road to the Bacas' house outside the mountain village of Las Trampas and handed Yvonne Baca a faxed letter from the California Department of Corrections. Yvonne waited until the deputy drove away, and then read the letter to her husband, Teófilo:

> As inmate's stated next of kin and person(s) to contact in the event of emergency we hereby inform you that inmate Faustino James Baca has been hospitalized in critical condition at San Francisco General Hospital following injuries sustained in a disturbance at the Soledad Correctional Training Facility . . .

As she read, Teófilo's legs began to tremble with the same hollow weakness he felt after a day of hauling logs up a steep mountainside. "Asesinos hijos de puta," he whispered, grop-ing for a chair. "Cobardes."

Yvonne took her red rosary beads from their lacquered box and knelt before the retablo to pray. After a moment, Teófilo pulled himself up and ducked into the tiny bedroom to change clothes. He pushed his still-shaky legs into his new Wranglers and chose his best buckle, the massive nickel one etched with his family name, Baca. He put on his black yoke shirt; its pearl buttons snapped in his head like distant gunshots. He brought his black boots and a jar of cracked old polish from the closet and polished the boots with slow, deliberate strokes, trying to calm his mind.

When the boots were polished, he reached up into the space behind the smoke-darkened third viga and took what was left of his earnings from the last four cords of wood he had cut. He slipped the money into his sock and pulled on his boots, rolling the legs of his jeans over them tight as bark on a log.

"That's only enough money for one to fly," Yvonne said. "And then maybe only one way."

"We could take the Greyhound."

"The Greyhound takes two days. By then . . ." She didn't finish. "You should drive down to Albuquerque and get the next plane," she said decisively.

"Yes," he said, adjusting the horsehair band on his felt hat to hide the worst of the moth paths. Twin hearts beat in his temples when he put it on. "But you'll need the truck while I'm gone. You drive with me to the airport and bring the truck back."

Yvonne flicked a brush over her tight black curls and was ready.

Teófilo had often wondered about the silver splinters that arced across the immense sky above Las Trampas and sank into the setting sun like falling sparks. It was difficult to imagine people sitting up there the way Yvonne had told him about, calmly drinking coffee and watching movies. But today, as they wound their way down into the Española Valley in the old Chevrolet, he wasn't thinking about planes or the flight he was about to take; he was brooding over the letters Faustino, his only brother, had sent them from Soledad prison.

The first letter, which was the first news Teófilo and Yvonne had had of Faustino since Teófilo had kicked him out of the house, coldly advised them where he had ended up. Other, more conciliatory, letters followed, sometimes wrapped in paños, big handkerchiefs on which he had drawn detailed pictures of hourglasses, prison bars, and butterflies. These letters detailed the complexities of prison life — the protection rackets, the racial hatreds — using slang that Teófilo did not always understand. They also proudly dismissed Teófilo's offers to go out to visit him: Faustino assured his brother he would be out on parole soon.

But in his last letter, which Teófilo and Yvonne had received only two weeks ago, Faustino practically pleaded with them to come to his parole hearing so that the board could see he had good and caring relatives.

"The Crip mayates call me rata, bro," Yvonne read. "And since I'm not into gangs, I don't get no protection from La Familia or La Eme. If I don't get out of here soon, my ass is grass."

Rata. Teófilo heard the word like a stab to his heart, not only because he knew it to be a serious charge among prison inmates, but because it happened to be the very word, spoken by Faustino in a completely different context, that had so enraged Teófilo the day he asked his brother to leave.

Teófilo had been in the yard that morning splitting fragrant cedar and yellow ponderosa when his brother emerged from the sagging little cabin, yawning and scratching. Faustino, whom Teófilo and his wife had taken into their home until he got his life together, squinted at the heaps of firewood and scrap lumber.

"Vivemos como ratas piñoneras, carnal," he said. "We live like wood rats."

Teófilo made no reply. But his aim was off the rest of the

morning, the misses glancing off the wedge, sending their sharp ring through the canyon as they scraped brilliant new wounds on the head of the sledge. Finally, after one stroke missed entirely and shattered the wooden handle, he marched into the house and told his brother:

"Agarra tu camino, hermano, largo de aquí. We got no use for you."

And Faustino was gone before Yvonne came back from the Furr's supermarket in Española with the week's shopping.

"But you know he says tonterías when he's going through detox," she told Teófilo, gazing dejectedly at the big white slabs of menudo she had gotten especially for Faustino. Menudo, with lots of chile pequín, was one of the best things for hangovers and alcohol abuse. "You're too sensitive, Teo."

Teófilo knew she was right. Faustino's brain was not yet dry; it was still soft and fofo like rotten heartwood. But he was still angry: "I don't give a shit! If he thinks the life of a woodcutter is so fucking bad . . . fuck him! Let him go back to stealing! 'We live like rats,' he said."

"At least he said 'we,'" Yvonne had murmured.

If the day when Faustino had left was clear and limitless, today was the opposite, the leaden sky soldered low and tight onto the horizon. Chícoma Peak across the valley was a solid triangle of snow. Teófilo glanced behind the seat to make sure the tire chains were there, and they were, bunched like a ball of steel snakes. Beside them lay a rusted old wood-splitting wedge, and the two of them together, wedge and chains, reminded him of a dream he had had in which his brother, having escaped from prison, came to him in shackles, and Teófilo freed him of them with a single blow of his sledge-driven wedge.

Yvonne knew how to put the tire chains on, even in the dark, and it would be dark when she drove back from Albuquerque. She was very capable. Much more capable, he often thought, with a kind of fearful love, than he.

And far more knowledgeable about the world. Sometimes her greater knowledge shamed him, but right now he was not ashamed to ask her what he had wanted to ask when she had read him that last letter from Faustino.

"Prieta, what is Crip?"

"It's a gang," she replied. "Crips and Bloods. Those are gangs."

"And what is mayate? What is that?"

Her dark complexion deepened. "It means, you know, Black. It's a bad word for a Black man."

Teófilo thought about the first and only Black man he had ever seen. It was at the Furr's in Española. He was a large man the color of Río Grande basalt, with hair so short it looked like lichen. Teófilo followed him discreetly around for a while to see what he bought: nothing unusual at first, just chips and Cokes, but then the Black man picked up a long package of pigs' feet, and that gave Teófilo a strange feeling of solidarity with him: Anglos never bought pigs' feet. Teófilo noticed then that the chocolate-shirted Furr's security officer, an hispano, was also following the Black man around, and anger flashed in him that this cop was hassling a brother. Then he caught himself: what did he, a wood man from the sierra, really know about these things? After all, Faustino's letters from prison made it seem that Blacks were natural-born criminals.

On I-25 south of Santa Fe, Teófilo let his eyes dart to the barren plains to the east, where the Penitentiary of New Mexico was said to lie. He could see no sign of it, though, and could only imagine it sitting out there in the darkening emptiness, a crowded den of restless men behind a tangle of barbed wire. He imagined all the various tribes swarming in there, the ones his brother had told him about: cholos, mexicanos, mayates, Apaches, mafiosos, bikers. At times he had had almost a kind of envy for his little brother's knowledge of this complex society; but now he could only think of it as a nest of rats turning on each other, as rats from different tribes always did.

It was evening rush hour in Albuquerque, the traffic tight and tense, cutting in front of him, riding his tail. Forced to stay in the middle lane, he nearly missed his exit to the airport and kept going to Belén. He swerved onto the looping ramp at the last moment, bald tires squealing. The car behind him, a small red sports car, blared its insulting horn at him. Yvonne caught her breath, perspiration bloomed under his arms, and for an uncontrolled instant the pickup slid toward the dusty little cemetery that lay below the ramp like a collection of a hundred forgotten roadside descansos, before correcting itself.

The airport signs baffled Yvonne: long-term parking/short-term parking/baggage claim/departures/arrivals . . . a barrage of arrows.

"Take — " She hesitated. "Take that lane!"

Teófilo swung into the lane to his left. Before them loomed a concrete portal, some of its entrances lit with green lights, others with red. The incoming cars jockeyed to the green ones, where drivers snatched cards from metal boxes. Striped bars rose and fell, letting the cars into the hulking garage.

Yvonne could not make out the words on the dimly lit box. "Let me see if I have change," she said, hunting in her purse. "Maybe it wants coins."

The car behind them gave a long blast of its shrill horn. Teófilo glanced in the rearview: it was the little red sports car again. A Black man in a fur coat leaned out of its window. His bald head, sticking up from that feathery coat, looked like a turkey vulture's.

"Hey, cowboy, what the *fuck* you doin'? What the *fuck* you doin'?"

Teófilo's heart stopped, as if to gather strength for the next beat; and when the next one finally came, it jumped into his throat and exploded there, strangling his curse.

The Black man swiped the air in disgust, careered into reverse, took another lane. The bar rose smoothly for him, and he hurtled into the garage, the screech of his tires echoing jeeringly from the darkness.

Yvonne leaned into her husband's trembling body to scrutinize the box again. "Déjalo, Teo, forget it, it's not worth it," she murmured. She reached over and pushed the button, and a ticket popped out like a mocking tongue. She yanked the ticket and the wooden bar rose.

The mayate's insults ringing in his ears, Teófilo experienced the same weakening in his legs he had felt after Yvonne read him this morning's letter. His shaky foot released the clutch too abruptly, and the pickup bucked and stalled. Yvonne threw her arms over her face as the bar came down with a thud on the windshield.

Teófilo did not punch the button again or get out to try to lift the bar. Instead, he turned the engine back on, revved it, and drove forward. The wooden bar bent against the windshield post and gave with a sharp and satisfying snap, like the brush he sometimes had to drive through on a long-abandoned lumber road. Yvonne gasped and glanced around, but no one was behind them now and no one seemed to have noticed.

Travelers thronged the terminal. Yvonne hurried to a row of TV screens. "Here. America West. Departure to San Francisco in, let's see . . . twenty-five minutes! Let's go, Teo."

She led him to a ragged line of passengers. A weary Anglo family in front of him nudged their enormous bags forward with sneakered feet. He stared down at his boots. "Cowboy," the mayate had called him.

Yvonne asked the harried, pink-cheeked woman at the counter about the next flight to San Francisco, and the woman typed crisply on a keyboard and said, "Yes, we have one seat available; how would you like to pay for that?"

Teófilo had forgotten to take the cash from his boot ahead of time, as he had planned to do. Now he cocked his left ankle over his right shin and tried to work the boot off as fast as he could. Yvonne grabbed his leg to help. Groans from impatient travelers rose behind them. At last they got the boot down far enough to extract the limp wad. The woman at the counter counted the bills disdainfully with her carmine fingernails.

His face burning with shame, Teófilo hobbled aside and braced himself against the counter to pull his boot back on. In the midst of his struggle he glanced up and met an audience of faces, some amused, some curious, others merely bored. And there, in the middle of the adjacent line, laughing with a blond girl, fur coat and shirt open to midchest to reveal a broad curve of pectoral muscle and a massive gold chain, stood the Black man.

Neither the blond girl nor the Black man was looking at him, and later he would come to believe they had not been laughing at him at all. But at the moment he was sure they were. He jammed his foot down hard, and the boot twisted to the side, throwing him off balance.

He heard his wife's voice as if through a bank of fog: "Gate 5-A, Teo."

The boot popped into place at the same time that his rage and humiliation locked in to a purpose. "Wait here," he told her hoarsely, and disappeared toward the garage.

He remembered something his brother had written: "Aquí en la pinta, el que madruga, la gana, bro. You got to get a jump on your enemy." Which is how they had gotten Faustino, no doubt. They had sneaked up on him. Le madrugaron. The other inmates would have turned their backs on the attack, saying nothing for fear of being branded ratas themselves.

Teófilo made a beeline to his truck, knowing where it rested among the other vehicles as surely as he knew where a given tree lay in the forest. He rummaged in the darkness behind the seat for any kind of makeshift weapon. Shanks, Faustino called them, something like that. He found the splitting wedge next to the tire chains. A rusty five-pounder. It felt good and familiar in his hand. He slipped it into the front pocket of his coat and strode back to the terminal.

He glimpsed a flash of fur disappearing into the men's room like a wild animal. He started after it, eyes hot, hand sweaty on the wedge. He imagined his brother being stabbed over and over by the mayates in a dim, shabby prison latrine, the tiles cracked, the blood pooling in the trough with the piss. And now Teófilo imagined himself driving the wedge into this mayate's black skull, the way cattle are stunned to death.

But he was unable to follow him into the rest room. He remained outside its doors, cold and shaking. It was with relief that he saw his wife approach.

"Teo, where have you been?" she asked. "We got to hurry. The plane's about to go!" She looked into his sweating face. "Ay, Teo. Ay, Teo. It's going to be okay. Faustino's going to be okay. But you got to go now. You have to go see him."

She steered him down the crowded corridor. The security men at the checkpoint told him to put his belt buckle, and everything metal in his pockets, in a plastic tray. Dazed, he drew his belt through the loops of his jeans and rolled it up and placed it in the dish. Then he took the wedge from his coat and placed it beside the belt. The men stared at it.

"He's a woodchopper," Yvonne explained quickly. "He forgets he's carrying it."

"Forgets he's carrying *this*?" said one of the security men, the Black one, hefting the wedge in his palm and laughing.

"Yes, he forgets he carries it," she insisted, but she was looking at Teófilo strangely. "Just keep it here and I'll be right back for it," she told the men.

The Black man made a chopping motion with the wedge, like a caveman with a hand ax, and laughed again, shaking his head.

Teófilo looped his belt back on. Now he wanted to laugh too, crazy-man laughter. He wanted to snatch the buckle off his body, this buckle that read, "Baca," and with a yell of insane glee, hurl it down the corridor so it could be trampled by this mass of purposeful and competent city people. Because fuck the Bacas, right? Fuck the Bacas and the horse they rode in on, these fuck-up people from the nothing village of Las Trampas, New Mexico. All of them fools, pendejos, a whole line of pendejos beginning with the first Bacas the valley people sent up there to fight off the Comanches trying to come across the mountains. Now they were nothing but wood rats and criminals. Las Trampas de los Pendejos should be the full name, the Trap of Fools. So laugh, all you gringos and all you mayates, you have a right.

"¿Teófilo? ¿Amor? You got to board now." Yvonne handed him a plastic orange card. Then she held him to her. "Ay, Dios mío. Oh, my God. Give my love to Faustino. If you need me to come out, call Tía and leave a message. ¿Bueno? I can get the money."

And then she was gone.

The plane was nearly full. A flight attendant guided him to his seat and buckled him in like a baby. It was a seat by the window, but he couldn't see anything outside, only a dull blur of himself.

A moment later he heard a man's big, friendly voice boom down the aisle, and then a heavy figure sat down beside him. A volley of exotic scent hit him. He cracked his tear-dampened eyes. It was the Black man in the fur coat.

"Oh, man, this traveling just wipes me out," groaned the man. "I just about missed this little old flight." He shifted his weight. "Hooee. Well. Hey, I'm Reginald King." Awkwardly from his cramped position, he stuck his many-ringed hand into Teófilo's chest.

Teófilo's heart thrashed, but he remained paralyzed in his seat, trapped and helpless. Anger sparked in the Black man's eyes when Teófilo did not reach for his hand, and then faded when his gaze dropped to the worn felt hat in Teófilo's lap.

"Oh, yeah, okay, now I get it," he said, and leaned heavily back in his seat. "Just my luck."

The plane began to taxi and the man spoke again. He spoke in a murmur, looking straight ahead. "You know . . . people in the city, in the urban life, go crazy. It's a crazy life, man. You yell at people in traffic. You yell at people you don't know. People you don't know, and you think you'll never see again. It's the freedom of being anonymous, know what I'm saying? It's crazy, man, crazy." He rested his head on the headrest and closed his eyes. "Oh, man."

The pilot's voice crackled over the intercom to announce that they were awaiting clearance for takeoff. Then the Black man spoke again, softly, eyes still closed.

"You're from, how'll I say it, the country, right? I'm from Oakland, California. Sometimes I think, damn, what would it be like to be from a rural place, where you know everybody, their whole family, everything that's happened to them. You know what they've been through, and you learn to be careful about what you say. The only time I learned to do that was when I was doing time, you know, in prison, where you know you're going to have to see, every day, the guy you just dissed. And then you get back into the outside, and you forget again . . . know what I'm saying?"

The shrill of the jet engines grew, and the plane moved forward and gathered speed. Teófilo sensed a strange gathering in some centerless center of his body, and then something, like the tender finger of God, pressed into his heart, and calmed it.

The Black man put his hand out again, pale palm cupped and facing upward. "Hey, look, my man, I'm sorry about all that in the garage out there. All right? Okay, brother?"

The plane lifted from the ground, and Teófilo felt a tremendous release. And though he knew this was the effect of their becoming aloft, he was sure, too, that this is what it felt like when the soul left the body upon death.

In front of him, against the dark blue of the seat, remained that outstretched hand, warm and waiting.

Archangela's Place

I watched them from the window, the two little naked boys. They stood together on the beach, gazing at the waves, their brown bellies protruding, the littlest one, who was about four, tugging absently on his foreskin. The older one was probably six. I was twelve. I was an only child and had rarely seen another boy naked, and never an uncircumcised one. I was duly amazed.

"What do you see there, buddy?" said my father, ducking his bristly, narrow head next to mine.

The bigger boy, without touching himself, let out a stream of urine, as nonchalantly as a horse, and the little one followed suit.

"Well, I'll be," my father said. I could practically feel his darkening glow on my cheek.

My father was a tall, scalpel-thin, unhappy maxillofacial surgeon. Though successful, he was weary of his profession, which for the most part involved pulling wisdom teeth, by his own admission a generally unnecessary operation. His Wisconsin therapist had agreed that a radical change of location and climate might help his spirits, so he had moved his practice from Appleton, Wisconsin, here to Southern California. To make the move more palatable to my mother, who had deep roots in Appleton, he gave her carte blanche on all domestic decisions. It was she, then, who chose this house, this many-cornered, many-leveled structure that had once been featured in *Ranch and Coast* magazine. "A metaphorical house," the article said, "organized symbolically by the forces of the sea." My father called the place "weird."

He clumped down the flagstone stairs to the "southern pavilion," where my mother sat indolently in a rhomboid of California sun. I followed discreetly behind. Out the tall Palladian windows we now could see a young brown-skinned woman, one of her feet planted firmly, boldly, unmistakably within our territory.

In the short time we had lived in that house, I had observed that everyone else knew by instinct where our private patch of sand ended and the public beach began. A foul volleyball, for example, would plop onto our property and the player would say, "Sorry," often without even glancing up to verify whether anyone was there to hear it. But this woman stood with her right foot unremorsefully in our, in Henderson, country: a foot wide and dark, shod in a cherry-red plastic sandal, the kind the girls at school called "jellybean" sandals. She wore a knee-length aquamarine skirt; her calves were as bronze and sturdy as a statue's.

"Christ. You know they come up here just to sit on the dole and screw and have more kids," my father told my mother.

"Brian?" she said, sensing my presence. It was a voice that warned I shouldn't be listening. But I lingered, out of sight, on the steps: I had to hear this business about screwing.

"It's the welfare state," he went on. "Pretty soon we'll have all of Mexico living in our backyard." He jerked open the sliding glass door. "Hey! Vamoose! Vamoose!"

The young woman turned and drilled him with wickedly beautiful sloe eyes set in a wide, high-cheekboned face. She kept one hand on her ample hip and touched a silver earring with the other. The boys studied him impassively.

"Vamoose!" my father repeated, making an exasperated shooing motion.

She moved languidly toward the surf, followed by her cubs. She waded into the waves and, gripping each boy by the arm, splashed water on his hindquarters and scrubbed him vigorously with her bare hand.

"Do you understand what I mean about the invasion, Maureen?" my father said.

"Well," my mother serenely replied, "we *are* close to Mexico, Leonard. I guess you knew that when you decided to move down here."

My father glared at her.

"So, then," she said, "trying to drive them off won't work. We have to welcome them, teach them *our* ways, and make use of them."

And with that she went out to talk to the woman on the beach.

Immediately upon our arrival in California, my mother had begun taking classes in Spanish, apparently in anticipation of hiring a Latin American maid (one of her textbooks was called *Home Maid Spanish*). Now, from the way her splayed fingers traveled up from her diaphragm, as if attempting to draw the stubborn words out, I knew she was trying her Spanish out on the woman. After a while she returned with a triumphant look. "Well, I could have told you. She's a domestic. And she's ready to begin anytime. She's even got local references."

"Christ!" said my father. "You can't hire someone right off the street. Or beach. And what about the kids? I'm not having a couple of Mexican rug rats running around here."

"Oh, golly, Leonard," my mother replied with a dismissive wave, "they can stay with relatives somewhere. Latins all have extended families. Her name's Archangela, isn't that cute? And, oh, she's so *personable*. I'd have introduced her to you now if you hadn't been so rude to her."

Archangela's references must have checked out, because I soon found myself helping my mother furnish the one-bedroom apartment she now called the servants' quarters. This unit, partially hidden by oleanders, sat directly across the far cleavage — the "butt," I called it — of our trefoil-shaped pool. We went to a used-furniture store and brought back a hideous black enameled bureau with a tarnished built-in mirror, an old spring bed, a small tile table, and a couple of brass standing lamps. For a chair we stuck in one of our canvas beach chairs.

"So her kids aren't coming?" I asked.

"No. Your father doesn't want them around, and frankly neither do I."

Her words wounded me. As an only child, I had always harbored the suspicion that I, too, was not wanted, that I was perhaps the result of an "accident," or an experiment my parents did not care to see repeated. I had no proof of this, of course, other than my only-ness itself, and what I perceived to be their emotional distance from me. At my father's funeral four years later, my mother confessed to me that they had always deliberately (perhaps too deliberately, she admitted) tried to avoid lavishing the kind of attention on me that would turn me into a typically spoiled only child. It was difficult, with an only child, to juggle the roles of authority and camaraderie, she said. But even with this explanation, I could still only resent them for their aloofness. Only when I ran away from home after the funeral and learned, on that trip, what had become of Archangela did I begin to forgive them. But now I'm getting ahead of my story.

My father had already left for his office when Archangela arrived, hauling all her worldly goods in two large Mexican shopping bags made of the same coarse canvas as our beach chairs. She smelled of candles and herbs and a hint of fish, and was dressed in the same aquamarine skirt and jellybean sandals that she had worn on the beach that day, and the same pair of silver filigree earrings dangled from her lobes. Thick rings adorned her bronze fingers. Her upper central incisors (my father always insisted I call teeth by their correct names) were edged in gold, and she had about the easiest smile I'd ever seen. She beamed. I was dazzled.

Archangela did not conform to any of my stereotypes of a maid. She wasn't the dour-housekeeper type, nor the rheumy-eyed, timid girl known generically in Mexico as "la muchacha." Mary Poppins? Well, certainly not the mawkish, plastic Julie Andrews Mary Poppins. She was as real as Alice of *The Brady Bunch,* except much younger and prettier and of course more exotic. But who was she, really? One day, thinking she was tied up with my mother in the kitchen, I sneaked into her room to see if I could get a clue.

The room was dim, the curtains drawn. It smelled resinously of her herbs and candle tallow, like some mysterious cave. Two little papier-mâché monsters faced off on her table; in front of them sat a fat candle in a glass and a smug little golden Buddha, and next to the Buddha, a tiny pewter bowl containing grains of rice. A resplendent Virgen de Guadalupe was pinned to the wall by her bed; beside it, an iridology chart, showing all the elements of the personality in the shards of an enormous lavender-blue iris. I was studying this chart when she came up behind me and touched my neck. I jumped a mile.

She reached over and drew the curtain above the bed and gazed into my frightened blue eyes. Her own pupils were drops of darkest ink in her nearly black irises.

"I want a child with eyes like yours," she murmured in Spanish. I understood only the words "ojos" and "niño," but that is what I think she said. She took my hand and placed it on her flat belly. My fingers felt warmth radiating from her breasts. I stood there stiff, with a helpless feeling I'd never known before, a kind of delicious and terrifying sailing into a vastness. Her nipples outlined her orange satin blouse, an inch from my mouth. I was expecting her other hand to come around and draw my head to her; and as my ear would listen to the thumping of her strange heart, the dryness of fear would recede from my mouth, and my lips, ever so slowly, would begin to draw moistly around one of those warm nubs . . .

But this did not happen. Not, anyway, until in my first wet dreams a few months later. She let go of my hand and I backed away, feeling that strength-in-weakness, weakness-in-strength that follows a rush of adrenaline. How I got from her room to the beach is a blank, but I remember sitting for a long, long time on a dune, far from the house, feeling the ocean's raw immensity down to my bones. Had I been inside one of the CAT or MRI scanners at my father's hospital, it would probably have revealed a bursting of hormones far more complex than mere adrenaline: the first trigger of my trigger's trigger, the first secretions of the coming Big Bang of my puberty.

"No limpia bien," Archangela said disdainfully one day of the washing machine. She beckoned me with a downward motion and stroked a stain on my shirt, just below my heart. A thrill ran through me.

"Oh, well, that's some kind of grease," said my mother. "That won't come out. No es posible. No preocuparse, Archangela."

But the next day the stain was gone. In fact, all the laundry came out resplendently clean, with a high-seas fragrance. The sheets, which Archangela wrapped on our beds with nautical tautness until my mother, who thought they should hang over the sides, corrected her, sailed me those nights into a delicious oceanic sleep.

I soon discovered where Archangela was doing the laundry. She was taking it down to the stream, where she met two other Mexican maids with their own loads. They smacked the laundry on the water, scoured it, slapped it on the rocks to dry, all the while yakking and screaming with laughter. I crouched behind a rock and spied on them, mesmerized by the smooth motions of their bodies. On one occasion, Archangela slipped out of her skirt and balloon-sleeved blouse and slid behind a rock to bathe: I glimpsed her bare arms, her shoulder blades working like embryonic wings beneath her tawny skin, her breasts, tinted green by the shadows of the vegetation, the size and shape of those big California avocados she was convincing us to like.

One morning, when my mother was once again marveling at the cleanliness of the clothes, I blurted my discovery to her, not anticipating the repercussions. My mother scolded Archangela and forbade her to wash in the stream. It was a nasty, primitive practice, she told her. She would have to use the washing machine from now on, whether she liked it or not.

I suspected that Archangela knew I had squealed on her: I caught her narrow eyes cutting into me with mistrust. To try to regain her affection, I stepped up my English "lessons," which consisted of my pointing out things and naming them, an activity she found hilarious. For a special session, I got her to walk on the beach with me so I could name things there. A crab, its eyes moving on their stalks, peered at us suspiciously from behind a rock.

"Crab," I said.

"Is you nahual."

"My what? What's a nahual?"

"You animal. You is crab." She waved her index fingers on either side of her head, imitating those all-seeing eyes.

"I'm not a *crab*," I said petulantly. But I knew then that she knew I had spied on her at the stream and had tattled.

The next day, I caught one of the handsome iridescent

beetles that buzzed along the stream, and brought it to Archangela. She appraised the beetle back and front, prized between her strong fingers, then kissed me on the forehead and dropped it into a baggie. The next day she was wearing it: she had run a pin through its underside and had glued little rhinestones to its wings. There it was, pinned to her bosom, its legs moving sluggishly, vainly. My mother shrieked.

I swore I would never squeal on Archangela again.

But, in fact, I did. It happened like this:

When the warm months came, Archangela asked my mother if she could sling a hammock on the beach behind the house and sleep outside, as was her custom in her tierra, the Isthmus of Tehuantepec. My mother was a little taken aback: she could not imagine sleeping all night in a hammock. I myself could not fathom anyone wanting to sleep out in the open, because to me, an only child, sleep was a very private thing; I hated spending the night at friends' houses, hated that feeling of vulnerability that came over me when the light of morning caught me in some strange bed, exposed to strange eyes. My mother advised Archangela of the possibility of "hombres malos" prowling the beach at night. She just laughed. Finally my mother relented.

If Archangela was an early riser, I was yet an earlier one, and I liked to creep outside and peep at her. I would find her sprawled slack-jawed and splay-legged in the hammock, her skirt hiked up to mid-thigh and her breast heaving with her whistled snores. As the dawn light turned from lead to slate, her snoring shut off, her dark eyes drew open, and she alighted from the hammock as smoothly as if she had been sleeping on a web of air. She would pad softly out to the surf and splash water onto her face. Then she would hold her skirt up and squat, and wash between her legs. Sometimes she sniffed her washing hand. Seawater, she had often told me, was a great tonic.

But I was not the only one to witness Archangela's morning ablutions. I once glanced up at my parents' window and saw my father standing there, gazing out at her, his pajama bottoms tented out in front of him.

At about this time — it was hot summer now — my father decided to take energetic night swims in the pool, nude. I could see him there from my upstairs window, his pale, strangely widened body shattered by the underwater lights. He favored the breaststroke: he was a giant albino frog. I sensed, not the least for the fact of his nudity, that this activity was a private thing, so I never went down to the pool then. I would just watch, lulled by the sight of his body gliding back and forth, broken kaleidoscopically by the water.

I had to wonder if my mother was ever troubled by his swimming nude so close to where Archangela lay, or if indeed she was even aware of it. She probably thought that being nude around servants was a sign of California sophistication; I remember her laughingly telling her new friends about her former diffidence toward servants, about how she used to tidy up before our cleaning lady in Appleton came over so the poor woman wouldn't have to step into such a mess. My mother's point being, if you couldn't be exactly yourself around them, and do exactly what you would otherwise do, as if they — no, as if *you* — were invisible, what was the point of having them?

My father swam, and I dreamed: wet dreams, as it were. In one of these dreams, my father sank like a stone to the bottom of the pool. I rushed out in my own nakedness to pull his lifeless body out, and as I did, my own body became powerful, rippling with a man's solid muscles. As I laid him out by the side of the pool, I saw how massive and hairy my own genitals had become. I rose and started toward the beach. As the surf crashed around us, I told Archangela what had happened, and she pulled me into her swaying hammock to stroke and console me. At this point I would awaken in my bed, lying in a puddle of sticky stuff that smelled like the chlorine my mother instructed me to sprinkle in the pool, or like the bleach Archangela used in the laundry room.

One night I awoke from such a dream and on the ceiling my gaze met the swirling golden striations of the pool lights. My father was swimming. I slipped out of bed, and crouched naked by the window, and watched his own nakedness. Back and forth he went. After a few smooth laps he rested his arms on the edge and looked up, scanning the windows of the house. I crouched lower. He pulled himself out of the water and sat on the diving board, his feet in the pool, the thick black hair on his legs limp arabesques, dripping.

The diving board emerged barbarously from between his legs. He glanced up at the house one more time, and then he pulled himself up and walked off the board, grabbed a towel from a chair, and strode around the redwood partition to where Archangela slept.

I remained in my crouch for a paralyzed moment, heart racing. Then I pulled on my shorts and stealthily negotiated the odd corners of the house until I gained the beach. There I saw two dim figures rutting on the sand like strange nocturnal sea mammals. I got down on my belly and slithered to the wall like a sidewinder.

"Ay, señor. Ay, señor." That husky voice was Archangela's.

I didn't hear my father's voice until the slapping of their bodies reached an urgent rhythm; and then it came out as short, sharp little barks, like those of a seal. It shocked me to hear these bizarre sounds coming from him. Archangela kept repeating "señor, señor," in a kind of counterpoint to the barks. When the noises stopped and he stood, I saw by her silhouette against the moonlit sea that she was on all fours, her rear high in the air, in the same posture she had assumed when she was down by the stream, scrubbing clothes. My father placed his foot between her legs and drew it back and forth. Her haunches rose higher, and finally she bucked and collapsed on the sand with a groan. My father remained there for a while, his foot on the small of her back, looking out to the sea like a fisherman with his trophy. He then ambled out to the surf and rinsed himself.

I fled to my bed and lay still but awake for hours, electrified.

I replayed that bizarre scene over and over again in my mind: the barking seal of him flopping over her, her cries, the astonishing episode with the foot. How, I wondered, could two beings who had done what they had ever look each other again in the eye?

But not only could they look at each other, my father started staying at home more, and Archangela would cook him special things.

"Papi eat here tomorrow?" she asked me one Saturday.

"I don't know," I said resentfully.

"I make," she said, puffing out her chest, "¡algo para hombre! Something for mens." She reached out to pinch or caress me, but I ducked. I couldn't stand her touching me anymore.

My mother helped Archangela grind the spices for this exotic new dish. In addition to Spanish, my mother was now taking courses in Mexican cooking; she and Archangela once prepared slimy cactus leaves in some sort of sauce, and more recently they had boiled an octopus together. Now they deboned a couple of chickens and made a broth, and then they set to grinding the spices: cloves and cumin and chile and coriander and pumpkin seed. They melted squares of bitter chocolate and added the broth and the spices and bread crumbs and kneaded the whole thing into a dense, dark mass, and let it sit in the refrigerator overnight.

"Chocolate chicken," I said the next day at the table, staring with disgust at the silver tureen with its gleam of white breast rising desperately from the luminous crimson surface of the sauce.

"Brian," my mother said to me in reprimand. She turned to my father: "Mole, it's called." And she recited its peculiar ingredients, trying to enlist my participation. I stayed mute.

"Sounds like an Archangela aphrodisiac," said my father, grinning maniacally.

"Leonard," my mother said, rolling her eyes in my direction.

I didn't know what an aphrodisiac was, but from my mother's tone I knew it was something sexual, and I was amazed at my father's boldness. I roiled inside with adolescent confusion and rage. I felt betrayed by everyone, including myself, my own feelings.

My father dipped his spoon into the sauce and tried it and choked. "*Holy* mole!" he exclaimed thickly, reaching for water. Archangela, her eyes merry, covered her gilded teeth with her silvered hand, and my mother laughed too.

My father ate it as if it were something dangerous but delectable. He said a bite of mole followed by a swallow of stinging beer tingled his brain and gave him the sensation that the top of his skull was being lifted in a peculiarly delicious way. I had no appetite at all.

"Too hot for you?" my father goaded me. "Come on, it's good."

Archangela kept him supplied with hot tortillas, cold beer, and pink rice. After gorging, he just sat there for a while, his eyes wet, his face purple, the corners of his mouth tinged red. He looked as if he might explode.

"Ah," he said, belching. "Better than a Perc."

My mother frowned, but it was the belch she was frowning at, not the reference to the "Perc." She was at that time oblivious to my father's problem with Percodan and Percocet, the painkillers that oral surgeons so often prescribe for their patients. It's a hazard of the trade, I learned after my father's death. She didn't even know what "Perc" meant — neither did I, of course — much less that one of its euphoric effects was this recklessness of speech. It occurs to me now that maybe it was the "Perc" that allowed him to so enjoy that painfully fiery dish. But all I knew then was that I hated the wet, sated way he looked at Archangela, and the way she beamed triumphantly back at him.

He turned his sweaty face again to me. "Not a bite, Brian? C'mon. You're not a sissy now, are you?"

I lost my head then. I leaped out of my chair and shrieked, voice cracking, "Leave me alone! You and Archangela can go to hell! I saw what you did with her!"

I ran to my room, terrified at what I'd blurted.

It took my mother the rest of the afternoon to sort things out. Archangela confessed sooner than my father. She added that she was pregnant.

That night I listened to my mother's normally calm voice fly and fall into heights and abysses as I had never before heard from her. Between the crashes of waves, I caught snatches of her argument with my father:

". . . a*bor*tion, Leonard?"

"If she *refuses,* god*damn* it? . . . can't *force* her . . ."

Finally, in the silence of the swelling sea, her voice came icy and clear: "Send her *back* to Mexico."

The next morning, my mother, red-eyed, hustled me off to school. By the time I got back, Archangela was gone.

I couldn't keep from thinking about Archangela pregnant with my half-sibling down in Mexico, a country that my parents had convinced me was one of unbearable poverty and depravity. I was sure, too, that this sibling would be born some kind of monster, if only because of the way it had been conceived — I was certain nothing healthy could come of Archangela and my father's unnatural coupling, and so large did the outrageous act I had witnessed bulk in my mind that I did not imagine they had had sex on any other occasion, or in any other way. Surely my mother and my father had never done it this way — or had they, and was I, too, some kind of monster? "Oh, go to Mexico, Archangela, go on!" I wept. "Go have your monster in Mexico!"

The following months were a time of tense and tentative healing in our family. It was the way a scab forms over a wound, at first pulling painfully on the tender skin all around it, and then becoming itchy, begging for someone to scratch it — talk about it — though no one does for fear it'll start to bleed again. So all mention of Archangela was studiously avoided. My mother became overly solicitous of me, while my father regarded me with an expression somewhere between quizzical and wounded. He blamed the affair on his abuse of narcotics and entered a detox program. At the end of six months, it seemed things were returning to as much normality as was possible after such an ordeal.

The scab, however, was torn off painfully the day Archangela showed up again on the beach.

I heard a soft chant: "Brian, Brian." A singsong, baby-soothing chant: "Brian, Brian." I looked out the window and saw her there, cradling a little caramel-colored infant.

She beckoned me with her downward wave, and I went, in a kind of dazed joy. I stared down at the baby's pinguid features, touched its wispy black hair. It wasn't a monster at all. Its eyes were half closed, but I saw they were as dark as hers. Archangela unfolded it for me, as she would a delicate fan, so I could see the length of it, and I saw its grublike penis. This baby, unlike his two little Mexican half brothers we had seen on the beach the day my mother had first spoken to Archangela, was circumcised, but years would pass before I understood the significance of this.

"You brother," she said.

The baby began to fret and she folded him back up. She glanced with misgiving at the house, kissed me quickly on the forehead, flicked the fringed edge of her rebozo over her shoulder, and strode down the beach.

"Who was that?" my mother asked sharply, stepping outside. She was pale.

"I . . . just a Mexican lady with a baby," I said idiotically.
My mother burst into tears and flew into the house.

That week my father brandished a pair of tickets from his
pocket: "Padres against the Giants, Sunday," he said, winking
at me conspiratorially. I winced; my father and I had never
even seen a baseball game together on television, much less
at a stadium; the invitation seemed so contrived and bogus. In
any case, we never got a chance to go through with this father-
son outing, because that Sunday morning, at about nine
o'clock, Archangela showed up again, this time right at our
front door. Again she had her baby with her, and she was accompanied by a wizened little rabbit-faced priest, her two
other boys, and a female friend or relative about her age. My
father, still in his royal blue bathrobe, answered the door.
Archangela, serene and smiling, asked him if he would like to
be present at the baptism of his son.

"Refugio, his name," she said, stroking the infant's wispy
hair. "Refugio Henderson."

Before my father could say anything, my mother, with a kind
of strangled shriek, rushed up behind him and slammed the
door in their faces. She locked it with a fierce twist and
stumbled upstairs, my father grimly behind her.

Upstairs, my father insisted that there was nothing he could
do about Archangela's being on the beach — *legal resident alien*,
he shouted, smacking his palm with his fist at every word. I
huddled in a corner of the southern pavilion and watched the
surfside baptism. Just a dab of water, touched with calm dignity to the wailing baby's forehead, just a drop from that immensity, whose slow beat had backed the urgent rhythm of his
conception, whose waters had been used in the furtive washing of his parents' scandalous genitals, was all that was needed
to make official my baby brother's spiritual entry into the
world.

*

My mother returned to Appleton, hauling me with her. When it became clear that she would never set foot in California again, my unhappy father followed us. He moved his practice back to Wisconsin, tried to get back together with her, but in the end she divorced him.

I lived with my mother, though I didn't stay home much. I started hanging out with a girl named Liz. What Liz taught me about sex made me regret that I had been so shocked at what I'd witnessed between Archangela and my father that night, and made me feel guilty about having squealed on them. But I displaced this guilt by feeling even more anger and contempt for my father: anger at how he had handled the Archangela affair after my mother, thanks to me, found out about it. I rallied all my adolescent feelings of righteousness and deemed it extremely cowardly of him to have agreed so readily to banish the pregnant Archangela to Mexico (somehow I could better understand my mother's hysterical demand that he do so) and then to have hightailed it back to Wisconsin and left her and my baby half brother to their own devices. I didn't know what I would have expected him to do, but I judged him harshly, as perhaps only a guilt-ridden adolescent judges an unloved parent.

My father, his blood molten with alcohol and painkillers, sailed his car off an icy bridge one night into a ginseng field, flipping it many times.

Not long after the funeral, I ran away from home with Liz. I was sixteen then, she eighteen. She had a Mustang ragtop. Our goal was Mexico, but we made it only to California.

I was not a happy travel companion on our trip west: moody and taciturn, I just stared out at the prairie, the mountains, the desert, playing the same Talking Heads tape over and over. I could tell Liz was thinking maybe this trip had not been such a good idea.

When we got to California, she said she wanted to see our

old place. "You gotta get back in touch with your past," she said. "Work through some shit."

I had told Liz nothing about Archangela or the events of those days, and I didn't want to now. "What for?" I muttered, gazing at the oleanders whipping by in the median. But as we neared the Pacific and I caught whiffs of its ancient salts, an undertow of dreadful nostalgia tugged at me, and I found myself telling her what exit to take.

I easily recognized the red tile roofs of the Mediterranean-style villa on the corner of our street, and the peach Georgian Revival house that signaled arrival at our own.

As we approached, I could smell the unmistakable fragrance of corn roasting in its shucks, and could hear brassy riffs of mariachi music from a radio.

Over a grill, which was nothing less than part of our wrought-iron gate set on a row of cinder blocks, stood Archangela, roasting the corn. The swimming pool was full of suds, and laundry lay drying around it. She stared at us for a moment, then broke into her dazzling smile and ran over.

"Little crab," she said, covering my face with wet kisses.

"My father's dead," I said. It was all I could think to say.

Her smile faded. "I know," she said.

A naked little boy of three or so with my father's weak chin and long legs bolted from the crazy shadows of the house, and with a gleeful shriek scurried for the greater protection of the former servants' quarters.

"Refugio," she said. "His nahual is rabbit."

Then, with a shriek of her own, she rushed back to the grill, where the ears had caught on fire, and slapped out the flames with her bare hands.

She beckoned us with that downward gesture of hers: "Come, come." Liz and I obeyed, and sat on a bench made from the pool's diving board and munched the deliciously scorched corn and listened to the surf and to the melancholy ranchera melodies and to Archangela's half-English, half-

Spanish chatter about her kids. We waited for them to over-
·come their shyness and join us, which at last they did. Refugio
stood before us and stared at us, playing with his penis. Archangela pointed to it and said, with a laugh, "Hombre gringo."

I blushed and looked out at the ocean. Liz, peeling another
ear of corn, said, "I think she means he's circumcised. That's
mostly an uptight gringo thing, you know. I don't think they do
it so much in Latin America."

An odd feeling of awareness grew in me as I absorbed these
words. I glanced at Archangela, who said, "Yes, your Papi . . ."
She made her fingers into an imaginary pair of scissors.

It occurred to me that if my father had performed Refugio's
circumcision, it was likely that he had cared for Archangela
throughout her pregnancy, and not packed her off to Mexico
after all. I saw then that my father was a more generous and
courageous man than I had ever given him credit for being. So
maybe my father had taken sexual advantage of Archangela; or
maybe she had taken advantage of him; or maybe all that was
irrelevant, maybe it just takes two to tango, as Liz liked to say,
and that's all there was to it. What was important was that he
had subsequently done his best by her.

This house, for example: apparently he had bequeathed it to
her. I knew he had won it in the divorce settlement — my mother,
too proud to contest or even discuss things Californian, had
kept the Appleton house and lake cottage — but I'd had no idea
that Archangela had ended up with it. I just assumed he had
sold it, and added the money to my trust fund.

Then I thought: perhaps, too, he had done his best by me.
Maybe I was within my rights to demand that he love me more
demonstratively; but maybe not. Maybe it was enough that he
had provided for me, which he always surely had. Maybe that
was love enough. For Archangela it plainly was. She seemed
happy.

All these things came to me in no more time than it took a
long, perfect wave to crash ponderously on the beach; and the

surf, pulling back, tugged from me an abrupt, ragged sob.

Later that night Archangela would sling a matrimonio-size hammock out back for me and Liz, and discreetly retire to the house. And that night I would, as the sea crashed behind us, tell Liz all about Archangela, and about our times here. I would spill my guts about it all and I would scarcely call it squealing.

Age of Copper

Every year on this date the electrical engineering firm where I work gives everyone the day off, uploads sensitive files to remote locations, locks and bars its doors, and hopes the street demonstrators do not lob Molotov cocktails through its windows. The date is September 11, anniversary of the 1973 coup that overthrew Salvador Allende and brought nearly twenty years of military dictatorship to Chile. The demonstrators, enraged at the military, say that despite "democratization" we continue to live under a kind of dictatorship. They point to the fact that General Augusto Pinochet Ugarte, who led the coup, is still head of the armed forces, still giving threatening, podium-pounding speeches at the Rotary Club, still celebrating the coup on this date with drink and song at La Estancia restaurant. Most of my fellow engineers are Olympically indifferent to politics, but none disputes the need to abandon the offices on this day, as word has gotten out that our firm sometimes contracts for ITT and other multinationals known to have funded the destabilization of Chile prior to the coup. We are, along with the carabineros, the police, and the multinationals themselves, a possible target of the demonstrators' anger.

I remain alone in my Santiago apartment this morning of the eleventh, reading. I leased it earlier this year, following my separation from the daughter of Admiral Móntez. Chile is one of the few countries in the world where divorce is not permitted, but after fifteen years of marriage to a woman I didn't love, and who didn't love me — it was virtually an arranged marriage, designed for the advancement of both our families — I finally worked up the courage to defy the opprobrium of family, church, and state, and left her. It was a decision in keeping with the times, in a sense — I feel I am democratizing my life, a life previously constrained by rigid and despotic values, opening it up to new and unexplored possibilities.

I understand that San Martín Street below is on the demonstrators' route as they make their way from Plaza Los Héroes to the General Cemetery, where Allende and hundreds of other victims of the coup are buried. As soon as I hear them surge into the street, I will go out to my balcony to watch. In my thirty-five years, I have never seen a demonstration, except on television. Today, though, I will be tempted to join them.

Since my separation, I have taken an interest in history and politics, particularly the history and politics of Chile. This interest has not been lost on my father, a General de Brigada Aérea. The other day, passing through Santiago on his way to the Parada Militar ceremonies, where every year he flies a Mirage, he gave me a book published by the U.S. Department of the Army titled *Chile: A Country Study,* no doubt believing it to be an antidote to more leftish treatments he has seen lying around my place. Today I peruse it with some skepticism, until one passage jolts me with its candor: "Even before Allende was inaugurated, a number of coups were attempted by right-wing elements within the armed forces. . . . Conservative, younger officers, horrified at having an avowed revolutionary Marxist as the nation's president, continued to plot throughout the three years that Allende remained in office."

My father was one such young officer. Implicated in the plot to assassinate the pro-Allende General Schneider, he was expelled from Chile in 1972, when I was twelve. He took the family — my mother, my two little sisters, and me — north to Colorado Springs, Colorado, U.S.A. The story he told nonmilitary people was that we escaped heroically in a liberated Hawker Hunter jet, the whole family piled in the cockpit, he at the instruments, nonstop to freedom. To fellow airmen, who knew you couldn't stuff that many people into a Hawker Hunter, much less fly it nonstop such a distance, he spoke darkly of our unceremonious dumping in Buenos Aires and of how we limped our way up on commercial airliners.

Colorado Springs was a natural choice: my father had been a foreign cadet at the Air Force Academy there and still had friends in the area. Moreover, the Rockies reminded him of the Andes, and the city was famously conservative in the generic North American sense, which meant we were less likely to encounter the decadence he felt was the sad legacy of American democracy.

We moved into a white clapboard house with green trim and a brilliant steel flagpole impaling the bluegrass lawn. Most of the families in our school district were military people or civilian employees at NORAD, the North American Air Defense Command. My junior high school was a squat brick building with slits for windows. My father laughingly called it "the bunker."

I quickly discovered that only three other students at the school spoke Spanish, three Chicanas with elaborately teased hairdos. I craved to talk to them, so one day I loitered around their gathering place behind the cafeteria. Soon they had me backed against the orange railing of the walkway. Pepsi, the tiny-waisted dark one with the especially big bangs, thrust a fistful of peanuts under my nose.

"So how do you call these in your Spanish?" she said.

"Maní?" I answered uncertainly.

Pepsi made her wrists go limp. "Oh, maní, my little maní."

"There's another word," said the big one, Carlota. "Say it."

"Cacahuate?"

They screamed with laughter. "You said caca!"

"And what are they in English?" The peanuts were damp in Pepsi's palm, the red skins wrinkled and soft.

"Peanuts?"

They howled. "You said penis!"

"So where're you from?" asked Pepsi.

"Chile," I said proudly.

They doubled over. Later I would learn that "chile" was Mexican slang for penis.

"And what's your name?" demanded the wide-faced one called Chata, wiping away a mascara-stained tear.

"José."

They went into a huddle, discussed this in whispers, and giggles broke around me again.

"No, your little name," demanded Carlota. "The one they call you."

"Pepe?"

"Pipí! Pipí!"

The prison-camp bray of the bell signaled the end of the lunch period, and I, trained by my father to be punctual, took off, feeling simultaneously offended by the Chicanas and grateful for their attention. But before I could make it to the classroom, two pairs of sneakered feet came gliding up behind me in the hall.

"We saw you talking spic with the putas," a twangy adolescent male voice murmured in my left ear, while a beefy hand twisted my right one. "We're on to you, freak. We don't care if your papa's some hot-shit pilot, you're just another greaser around here."

My slender, dapper father was young and self-confident, and had an effortless smile. He made friends easily. One of those friends was a bearish officer at the academy, one of my father's former instructors. This officer allowed my father to fly fighters, to "keep his wings sharp," as he put it. What I'm sure he didn't know is that my father sometimes snuck me along.

I dreaded seeing my father in his dark blue service uniform with its lighter blue Comandante de Escuadrilla insignia on the sleeve: it meant we were going flying. He would whisk me aboard the plane, strap me into the copilot's seat, slip as neatly as a shim into his own, and fire the fighter up. When the screaming engines reached their impossible highest note, we lurched to takeoff over the Rockies. The g-forces pushed the blood into my legs and feet until I thought my toes would pop. He did loops and rolls and my head snapped back, and I would black out for a moment; my organs crashed and churned inside me, and my eyes felt pressed into my skull as if by thumbs. While I clenched my teeth against the nausea and tried to concentrate on an imaginary point in front of me, solid and indivisible, he would blithely indicate the different mountains, Pikes Peak and Cheyenne Mountain and the Collegiates, shouting out their similarities to Aconcagua and Ojos del Salado and our other Andean peaks.

I was proud that I never puked until we got home. But then I'd have the dry heaves all night.

"Está malito," I heard my mother tell my father once as I rested my forehead on the cool rim of the porcelain bowl. "Bien malo."

"Malito no," my father laughed. "He's learning to be *machito*."

My mother did not directly ask my father to stop taking me up in the jets; a good military wife, she was reluctant to interfere in men's affairs, not least a father's relations with his son. I understand that in the United States a child can actually sue his parents for neglect or mistreatment — a preposterous idea in Chile — but it did not occur to me to even mention it to anyone outside the family, such as a teacher. In any case, it was unlikely that any of my teachers would have done anything about it, because most of them were politically conservative, which meant they, like my mother, would not want to intervene in what they would perhaps consider an acceptable rite of male initiation.

Among the most conservative was my Colorado history teacher, Mr. Roberts, a middle-aged man who wore a camel's hair coat that matched his eyebrows and his skin and his yellow-gray hair. At the end of class he would either read us a passage from an Ayn Rand novel or show us newsreels about Red China. We learned to shout "ugh" at the sight of Mao's wide Chinese face with its big chin mole.

His favorite subject was mining. The history of Colorado was the history of mining, he told us. Mining was also the history of such countries as South Africa and Bolivia. And of Chile, he said, fixing his yellow gaze on me.

One day he asked us to empty our pockets and identify the metals we carried there. Nickel, that was easy. But did anybody know what pennies are made of?

"Pennies or penis?" giggled Pepsi, who sat in the back next to me.

"Pendeja," I whispered.

"Pinche cabrón," she replied.

Mr. Roberts looked our way, his features an ocher blur. (I didn't know yet that I'd grown nearsighted.)

"José," he said, "what's your country's most important export?"

"Come on, you dumb spic," muttered the boy hunched in front of me.

Cobre. But I didn't know the word in English, so I sat there in silence.

Mr. Roberts scooped up the pennies I had laid on my desk. "Copper," he said, shaking them in his fist like dice. "So what else is copper used for, besides pennies?"

"Wires," someone said.

"That's it. Telephone wires. Copper is an excellent conductor."

He strode to the front of the room. "The country of Chile is one of the world's principal exporters of copper," he bellowed. "And the communist government of that country has seized control of it!" He slapped the pennies down on his desk with a crack like a gunshot. "If the free world doesn't get Chilean copper back, all communications will fall under complete communist control! You control communications, and you control the world!"

All eyes fastened on me with theatrical hatred.

"Mr. Braun," he said to me, pouring the pennies into a jelly glass. "I'll make a deal with you. You may have your pennies back when you decide to stop whispering things in Spanish in my class, or when your people give the world its copper back. Whichever comes first."

That night I complained bitterly to my parents about Mr. Roberts. My father told me North Americans were sensitive about Spanish being spoken behind their backs. The Mexican and Puerto Rican hordes were, after all, invading their country, and that made them nervous. For your own good, he said, stay away from Chicanos, don't speak to them, they are the low offspring of the Mexicans. They are the Mapuches of North America.

As for Chile, he said, the teacher was lamentably well informed. The communist Allende had taken over the American copper mines as well as the telephone company, and this, with reason, had made Kennecott and Anaconda and ITT and the U.S. government angry.

"But what about my pennies?"

"You'll get your pennies back," he said with that confident smile. "The communists will fall."

My mother nodded solemnly.

"But now the kids call *me* a communist!"

"Then defend your honor against such calumnies with these," he said, reaching across the table and curling my hands into fists.

Mr. Roberts taught us a complex abdominal mnemonic for remembering the geographies of some communist countries: populous Red China was shaped like a pregnant woman's *belly*; under it dangled the *umbilical cord* of North Vietnam, which nourished the *fetal communism* of South Vietnam. Cuba was a machete pointed at the *belly* of the U.S., which Castro in fact called "the *belly* of the beast." Chile, the latest country gone communist, was shaped like a hot chile pepper, and like a hot chile pepper, was giving the free world *indigestion*.

The next morning, the sneakered feet whispered up behind me in the hall and stepped on my heels. "Hey, Chile Lips, look what we have for you." A blond boy dangled a slender red chile pepper in front of my nose. "A little after-school snack."

I told the Chicanas about him. Their verdict was swift: "We gotta jump the cabrón." After school the three of them and I ambushed him along the creek that tumbled down Cheyenne Mountain. I had never been in a fight before. My body felt like something I could not control. We rushed at him from the scrub oak like wild peccaries and threw him to the ground. As he writhed, I tore into his pockets, searching for the pepper. "Fuckin' spics fight dirty," he gasped. I found the pepper. The Chicanas told me it was a chile de árbol, the hottest kind. I crushed it against his thin lips, hoping they would swell like my own, which were plump and red and not manly. He sputtered and spat at us. I rubbed his pale-lashed eyes with my red-flecked fingers and he screamed. We let him go and he rushed into the creek and thrashed his face in the cold water. We melted into the bush.

*

Recently I read that one of the many tortures practiced by the DINA, Pinochet's secret police, involved squirting hot-pepper solutions in prisoners' eyes, forcing it up their noses. After they got all the information they were going to get, the DINA would kill the prisoners. Many of these dead, as I said, are buried in the General Cemetery, which makes the cemetery a natural, if highly volatile, place for the march and demonstration to end. I believe I hear the demonstration approaching now, a far-off roar. I peer out the balcony's French windows, as far as I can see up the street, but I see nothing. The carabineros are ready, though; they have taken up positions in the entryways of buildings. I hear a rumble and then see a boxy armored vehicle with water cannon emerge from a cross street and stop at the corner.

I think about the savage way I rubbed the hot pepper into that boy's eyes, about the satisfaction it gave me, and it troubles me. Though it's not much comfort, all I can say is that I couldn't have possibly known about its similarity to the DINA's tortures, because the coup that overthrew Allende and put Pinochet and the DINA in power was still six months away.

"Let's ditch and cruise," said Pepsi one day at lunch, squashing a cigarette under her high heel. We sauntered down an alley and across the creek to her shabby house. Leroy, her older brother, was slouched in his toothpaste-green Impala, the Green Envy, smoking. He gazed impassively out the tinted windshield while she spoke to him. After a while he straightened up and the rest of us got in the car and we cruised downtown.

"That's where the Time Man lives," Pepsi said of the Mountain Bell building. It was a solid building, with metal doors and no windows, even more fortresslike than our school.

"Who's the Time Man?" I asked.

"Híjole," said Pepsi. "He doesn't know who the *Time Man* is!"

"That's because he's a Latino," said Leroy. "He don't give a fuck for gringo time." His bloodshot eyes glanced at me in the rearview. "Right, bro?"

"Yeah," I said uncertainly.

"You call up this number on the phone," said Pepsi, "and the Time Man tells you what time it is."

"But he won't never, ever talk to you," said Chata.

"He's the most powerful dude in the world," said Pepsi. "He controls the time. He sits in there by himself with a clock and a thermometer. All by himself in that building. You can call him, but he won't ever talk to you, except to say the time and the temperature."

"Don't believe their shit, bro," Leroy said with a laugh.

I couldn't tell whether Pepsi and Chata believed it themselves or not. I believed it, though: in my country, jobs abounded where a human being was assigned a single, tedious service task — elevator operator, doorman, usher — and though I hadn't seen many people working such jobs in the United States, they surely had to exist. So I believed in the Time Man, and when I got home that day, I called him. His voice was firm and factual, very American. He seemed exceedingly sure of himself, of his knowledge, like Mr. Roberts, like all my teachers. After he spoke, it took him a long time to hang up, as if he was expecting me to say something.

"We got all the copper, fucker," I said the second time I called, my voice quaking, and hung up.

I rocked on the floor with frightened glee until it dawned on me that all telephone wires, including ours, went into the telephone building, and that he could trace where all calls came from and where all went. That was another reason he was all-powerful: he controlled not only time but communications as well. The rest of that evening, each time the phone rang, I jumped to intercept the call, believing he was phoning to turn me in to my parents. But the calls were all long distance from Washington or from Chile. My father took them in a low voice in his study. It was 1973 and serious things were happening in Chile, things to which I was then oblivious.

My father returned from Washington one night flushed with a mysterious exaltation. He asked me animatedly about school, asked me how things were going in Mr. Roberts's class. I told him I hadn't gotten my pennies back yet, and he laughed and said, "Soon, hijo, soon." I told him we were still learning about mining, and I described the old mining towns of Cripple Creek and Leadville and Silverton. He clapped his hands: that would be a great trip for us to take on the weekend, a tour of some of those places. After all, who knew how much longer we would be in Colorado? My mother looked at him inquisitively, and he winked at her and said: "Because times change, times change! It's just a matter of time!"

That Saturday we wound our way over Goldcamp Road, our headlights on as a sign of solidarity with President Nixon and in repudiation of the communists and hippies trying to oust him from power. We twisted around craggy Cheyenne Mountain and into the gouged and denuded hills of Cripple Creek. My little sisters got carsick, but I, hardened by having flown with my father, proudly did not.

I was also proud of my knowledge, and of the fact that my English was by now so good that I understood nearly everything Mr. Roberts taught us, and I repeated in eager detail the heroic story of how this mineral-laden land had come to be developed — of how the savage Ute Indians had to be driven off, the communist-run miners' unions crushed. I told everyone about how the National Guard had to be called in to smash Big Bill Haywood and his Western Federation of Miners in the early 1900s, and I told of the Ludlow Massacre, how the communist agitators had forced the National Guard to machine-gun and burn the tent city of striking miners.

My father listened intently, and said he was amazed at how similar this was to the history of Chilean mining. In our country, too, the Indians first had to be subjugated. The Mapuche, who had continued to resist the Spaniards throughout the colonial period, were finally driven onto reservations, and this allowed Chuquicamata, now the world's largest open-pit copper mine, first discovered by the Incas, to be excavated in peace. He told of similar labor troubles, of the massacre at Iquique, where two thousand rebellious peons had to be killed. The magnitude of the Iquique massacre, a hundred times greater than Ludlow, just proved how much bigger and more important our mining was compared to the mining here, he boasted.

And so we coiled our way over the high roads, almost Andean in their treachery, comparing facts, eating my mother's Chilean empanadas stuffed with plump raisins and spicy minced meat, remembering to turn off the headlights at every stop and on again as soon as we hit the road, a fun and educational trip on a bright, cool mountain day.

In those days, Pepsi's brother Leroy let me see her only when he was around. After school, and on those nights when I managed to slip away from home, we all cruised in the Green Envy. Leroy said he was into Chicano power. He said he was a Brown Beret, except he didn't have the beret yet. He thought it funny that my name was Braun, which was not a Spanish name, yet I spoke Spanish better than he, a Ramírez, and that despite my name my skin was not brown at all, at least not Toltec brown like his. Leroy said I was a brother anyway. Brother Braun who is not so brown.

"And you," he said to his sister. "Why do you let them call you Pepsi? Oh, yeah — because you're dark and bubbly. But Pepsi Cola, that's the black waters of Yankee imperialism."

Leroy wanted to know what was going on in my country. Wasn't the CIA trying to overthrow the government, the way they tried with Cuba? Weren't they trying to kill the president, what was his name, Allende, the way they did to Che? And wasn't the telephone company ITT paying them to do it? That's what the Beret newspaper said.

I shrugged. I didn't know those things. All I knew was that my parents didn't like Allende or his government.

We cruised around the Broadmoor Hotel, once, twice, many times. Leroy said it was a bourgeois hotel. He said a Brown Beret brother had accused President Allende of being bourgeois because he liked fine wines. Did I think fine wine was bourgeois?

I didn't know what "bourgeois" meant, but I said it was probably bourgeois.

"Well," Leroy said after a while, "I like fine wine. I'm tired of Spañada." And he pulled into the parking lot of the elegant hotel.

"We'll get it," said Pepsi. "Come on," she said to me.

The gigantic, Prussian-looking doorman, who sported a high-collared tunic with epaulets like an admiral on Battle of Chacabuco Day, tried to give us mal ojo, but we proceeded boldly into the gift shop, where I distracted the personnel by demanding attention like a rich foreign brat, while Pepsi walked out with two bottles of champagne called Brut. Leroy, looking disdainfully over the booty, said Brut was the name of a cologne. But it tasted good anyway, and we drank one of the bottles as we tooled around Cheyenne Mountain.

"This mountain's hollow," said Leroy. "Did you know that?"

"Mines?" I said. I couldn't think of how else a mountain would be hollow.

"Not even, bro," said Leroy. "Under there, way under, there's this thing called NORAD. They watch everything that goes on in the sky. Everything. They're the most powerful people in the world, because when they say here comes a missile from Russia, then that's it. We send our own missiles and then everybody kisses their ass good-bye."

"No, the most powerful man is the Time Man in the telephone building," insisted Pepsi. "Because he controls the time. And his building is safe from bombs."

"Don't be tontita," Leroy told his sister. "If everybody in the world is blown up, it don't matter *what* the fuck time it is."

We got as far as we could up a side road until we were turned back by a fence and signs warning us not to proceed without authorization. When we were down in the oak-shrouded darkness again, Leroy pulled into a hidden turnaround, and said, "Let's fuck the cabrones up."

He took a long rope from Green Envy's trunk. He tied one end of the rope around a rock, then heaved the rock over the wires.

"Híjole, you're gonna get electrocuted!" Pepsi shrieked.

"Chale, these are telephone wires, not high tension," he said. "The high-tension wires run staggered. You would know that if you read the *Manual of the Urban Guerrilla* like I told you."

Leroy tied the rope to Green Envy's bumper, revved the engine and threw it into gear. The Impala lurched forward, came to a jolting stop like a carrier fighter with a cable on its tailhook, then shot forward again as the telephone wires snapped.

"¡Viva Chile!" shouted Leroy as we sailed down Cheyenne Mountain, the rope whipping behind us.

Leroy went by Der Wiener Schnitzel and picked up his girlfriend, Dora, who had just gotten off work. We cruised some more and finished off the second bottle of Brut, which was still as cold and sparkling as the stars over the mountains. Pepsi and I sat in the back. She put her warm hand on my leg, and my penis grew heavy in my jeans, like a roll of brand-new pennies.

The next day, Pepsi came over on her banana-seat bike to look for me. She was wearing a vanilla-cool blouse and tangerine

culottes, and her legs were like chocolate slightly softened by
the sun. We laughed about the night before, and she asked how
I felt today, and I said thirsty, and she said her eyes hurt. She
dared me to call and talk to the Time Man and I did. I said,
"Qué pasó, payaso," and then she talked to him, "Qué hubo,
bobo," and then she called again and told him we were sorry for
the insults but why didn't he talk to us, and after he hung up
that second time, I called back and said he might be a hot-shit
gringo but we still got the copper, cabrón, and then she called
and told him he'd better watch his wires because her brother,
Mr. Che, and her boyfriend, Mr. Pe, knew how to pull them
down, and when she said "boyfriend" a thrill ran through me
much different from the fear that had run through me that
time I had called the Time Man when I was by myself, and I
was not scared of him at all now. Then she jumped up and said,
"Let's go look for the wires."

So we grabbed two cans of pop and went up Cheyenne
Mountain Boulevard on our bikes, up and up, with light-bod-
ied giddiness. We looked for but couldn't find the place where
we had pulled down the telephone wires. Hot and panting, we
wheeled our bikes into the cool woods. We found a many-lay-
ered bed of oak leaves. We lay on our backs and watched a
squadron of screaming fighters leave five perfectly parallel
white trails. I rolled over and looked into her green eyes; they
glittered like the needles of the sun-drenched firs around us.
We kissed long and soft, and unbuttoned each other's clothes.
For a moment I thought of the men in the hollowed-out mountain on which we lay, wondered if they could see us, or hear us.
But in another minute I didn't care, and in the minute after
that I thought ah, the mountain has been hit, the world has
exploded, time has stopped, and it's only Pepsi and me, floating
through the universe on our patch of pungent ground, forever.

When I got home that afternoon, smudged with black soil
and smelling of humus and a new kind of sweat, my mother,

who had seen Pepsi wave good-bye to me on the street, looked at me crossly and said, "Of all the ones you could choose to be friends with, you choose the most Indian."

But for the most part that summer, the summer of 1973, my parents were too distracted by the rapidly deteriorating political situation in Chile to pay any attention to my activities. My father rigged a shortwave antenna to the roof, with a wire stretched to a tree for better reception, and he and my mother spent long evenings huddled around the radio in his study, listening to Spanish-language broadcasts about the riots and demonstrations and coup attempts. As my parents fretted and exulted over events in Chile, I took every opportunity to meet Pepsi in those oak-scented woods. Today, as I close my eyes against this cold and dreary September sky and recall that August in that other hemisphere, I conjure feelings of brightness and wonder that I must confess I have not felt since. Then I consider how things might have been had the coup in Chile not taken place and we had continued to live in the United States. Would my parents, giving up hope for any immediate political change in Chile, have centered their attention on their children and forbidden me from seeing Pepsi the Chicana? Would my resistance to them have turned me against them, even radicalized me and compelled me to join Leroy and his Brown Berets? Or would I have given in to their exhortations to conform, the way I later succumbed to the pressure to marry the daughter of Admiral Móntez? Would I have endeavored to be accepted by the rest of my schoolmates, become integrated into middle-class American life, played their brand of football, learned to speak like them, learned to shun outcasts like Pepsi and her brother? Both of these scenarios rumble through my mind, each holding the same weight of possibility as the other.

The coup took place on September 11, a few days after Pepsi and I entered ninth grade. I heard whoops and shouts from my father's study that night, and my parents rushed into my room, roused me from bed, hugged me: We're going home, going home!

I found Pepsi before school, standing behind the gym, smoking with Chata. I told them I was going back. At first, Pepsi took the news stoically, indifferently. But when Chata left she began to cry, her teased bangs bobbing with her sobs. We held each other for a long time and then decided to head off campus.

We ran into Mr. Roberts in the parking lot. "Bwaynos deeas, Señor Braun! And a mucho good day it is, too!" He held up the newspaper for me to see: COUP TOPPLES CHILE REGIME; ALLENDE REPORTED DEAD. He grinned a big, yellow-toothed grin, fished in his pocket, and brought out a handful of pennies.

"A deal's a deal!" he said.

"Give him his," said Pepsi, teary-voiced.

"What's that, señorita?"

"Give him the same money you took from him. The pennies in the jar."

Mr. Roberts looked at me and I stared back at him.

"Why, sure," he said. "You want the very *same* pennies. I can comprende that."

We followed him to his room, where he emptied the twelve pennies from the jelly glass into my palm. "Here you go. Doce copper pennies norte americanos."

"Cabrón," Pepsi said to him as we walked out.

Upon our return to Santiago, my father became a protégé of Air General Gustavo Leigh and would eventually rise to the rank of General de Brigada Aérea. He told nonmilitary people that he was one of the pilots that had strafed the Moneda, the presidential palace, during the coup. To the military people who knew better, he spoke only of the homesickness of exile.

My father enrolled me in an exclusive military school, where the other cadets treated me with respect. Ours was a caste cut off from the rest of the world, and I knew and understood little about outside society, except that it was my caste's duty to impose order on it. I knew nothing about the political prisoners, the disappearances, the torture — these things were not spoken of in our circles. Even the nightly curfew didn't strike me as particularly strange, and in any case it did not affect me, since I had only to call one of my father's military escorts to pick me up from school or a friend's house whenever I remained there after dark.

It was Leroy who got closest to informing me about what was happening in Chile. I had written to Pepsi once, a rambling, depressed letter, and given her my number, not expecting anyone to actually call. But one night I got a call from her and Leroy. They had broken into the junior high and were using the vice principal's phone. I talked to Pepsi and she said she missed me and I said I missed her. We were bored and lonely, we said, and we missed each other. Leroy, obviously impatient, got on the phone and asked if I could talk. Puzzled, I said sure.

"So what's the deal at the stadium?" he said.

"Stadium? Football, mostly. You know, what the gringos call soccer?"

"You can't talk," he said, and hung up.

I asked my father what games were happening at the national stadium, and he said, "It's no game. But if it were, let's just say the Reds have lost."

I didn't pursue the subject. Only years later would I learn that Pinochet's men had herded thousands of his enemies into the stadium, which served as a concentration camp following the coup. Many were killed there, their bodies thrown into the sea or buried in abandoned saltpeter mines.

Pepsi and Leroy's call was traced to our house. It was obvious to my parents that it had been made by "those Chicanos," so I was spared a lengthy interrogation. But I never heard from either one of them again, by phone or by mail — I suspected my

mother intercepted any letters. And when they disappeared
from my life, so did my connection with politics. Incredible as
it sounds, Leroy, that Chicano militant in Colorado, was until
recently my last reliable source of information about what was
happening in my country. I don't offer this as an excuse for my
political ignorance over these last twenty years, but it is a fact
that people living in dictatorships often have no idea of what is
happening under their noses. This is especially true of people
at the center of the dominant class, people like me, a general's
son who would soon become the husband of an admiral's
daughter, and whose profession, engineering, is notoriously
devoid of interest in the human.

I hear now a chanting of thousands, and my heart speeds up. I
venture out to the balcony and see them coming down San
Martín. All I have to do is slip downstairs and join them. My
neighbors are already out on their balconies, jeering. They'll
see me join them, and word will have it that the general's son is
a Red. I am not worried about them. I am more worried about
being arrested and what I will tell the people I am jailed with if
the police, to spite me, inform them that I am the son of a general. In my defense, I will be tempted to tell my comrades that
even before the coup, at the tender age of thirteen, I helped my
"cell" sabotage telephone lines as an act of resistance to ITT,
which I knew even then to be plotting with the military against
Allende. It would be an exaggeration, but not quite as flagrant a
lie as my father's boast of having flown his family to exile in a
Hawker Hunter during the Allende years and then returning
triumphantly to strafe the Moneda. But then I remind myself
that my father always told the bitter truth to his own people,
military people. And those people in the jail, they would be my
people then. And I would have to tell them the truth.

I don't have to join them. I can still dismiss the demonstration as a parade of dinosaurs, as most of my colleagues would.
As the fiber optics man who shares my office space does. He

likes to say the Allende years and the coup took place in the Age of Copper, a time in the distant past when the world's communications depended on that metal and governments were overthrown for it, a metal now being replaced by fiber optics, whose ultimate source is that timeless, eternal commodity, sand.

But he's a fool if he really believes this. The Age of Copper is not over, history is not over. The dictator has appointed himself Senator-for-Life, the company where I work still contracts with ITT, the bodies lie restless in the General Cemetery.

The voices grow louder. Another armored vehicle with water cannon zooms down the street, ahead of the march. Many of the marchers wear helmets — motorcycle helmets, construction hardhats. Some wear bandannas over their faces and carry long truncheons.

I go inside, leaving the French doors to the balcony open. I enter my study, which is where I keep a little copper box hand-hammered by the Mapuche. Inside the box are the twelve North American pennies Pepsi and I got back from Mr. Roberts. One of them is curiously dark for having been handled so little. This dark one carries the date of that fateful year, 1973. Every Chilean should own a dark 1973 American penny, I think. I think: perhaps I should take it with me, for luck.

Cosas, Inc.

It was ten o'clock on an April morning, the Taos sun already blinding on the pale stucco of my little bookstore. I shielded my eyes against the glare, managed to get the key in the padlock, but the heavy chain slipped through my shaky hands and cascaded with nerve-jangling clangor through the wrought-iron bars of the cancela. Head pounding, I hurried to the storeroom, grabbed a couple of empty boxes, and scurried back to the street to remove my books from one of the building's two adjacent display windows.

This window belonged to the building's other retail space, but the landlord allowed me to use it, as well as my own window, as long as I was the only tenant. Now new tenants, new neighbors, were due to move in that morning, and I wanted to have the window ready for them when they came. It had been a long and lonely winter for me, and I wanted to be hospitable and avoid giving them the impression that they were pushing me out.

I hauled the boxed books — travel guides to New Mexico and the Southwest, Tony Hillerman mysteries, the obligatory D. H. Lawrence novels — to my store, flung myself into my old swivel chair, poured myself a nip of the hair of the dog, and waited. A few minutes later, they pulled up in a white panel van. There were three of them: a tall, sandy-haired man and a black-eyed woman, both wearing jeans and plain white shirts, and a mahogany-dark young man — a boy, really — dressed in busily brilliant Guatemalan Indian costume. I took a deep breath and went down the hall to introduce myself.

The tall man could have been anywhere from my age — late twenties — to early forties. He held himself crookedly, as if his body had been broken and ill-fitted back together. His complexion was pitted and waxen, his lip sculpted in a fixed sneer above his eyetooth. He introduced himself as Ernesto Dreyfus. His wife, Susana.

"Jaguar jew," she murmured. I had to think a few moments to realize this meant "how are you?" The expression on her swarthy, round face was as reticent as her husband's.

The Indian carried an enormous burden of colorful clothing on his back, which he gingerly deposited on the floor by bending over backward and releasing the tumpline from his forehead. Seeing that the Dreyfuses were not going to introduce me to him, I stuck out my hand. He gave me a dead-fish shake, murmured his name — Archimedes — and dropped his timid gaze to his feet; they looked shriveled and cold in his enormous tire-soled sandals. Susana said something to him in abrupt Spanish, and he hurried back out to the van.

"Beautiful stuff," I said, rubbing the cochineal-red fabric between my fingers.

Susana gave me a tenuous smile, but Ernesto was scanning the room anxiously and didn't acknowledge my comment.

"Hey, how about a toast," I said. "Come on over to my place; we'll toast your arrival." I raised an invisible shot glass to my lips. "Tostada? Tequila?"

"Ah," said Ernesto, his look of puzzlement becoming one of pain. "Ah. Thank you very much. Yes. Later? Yes?"

"Little too early, huh," I agreed with mock guilt.

"Too early, yes, early!" said Ernesto. "Thank you."

They turned to each other and began setting up shop. The marimba over here, no, over there; all the blouses together and the skirts next to them; these trouble dolls will go on the counter. Their shingle went up: COSAS, carved in Gothic lettering. Cosas — Things. Not very catchy, I might have told them, had they asked my opinion, which they didn't. Indeed, they asked nothing of me at all, or about me, or about my shop, or the building, the landlord, Taos, nothing. They ignored me.

"So how'd you guys get into this business?" I finally asked.

They glanced at each other and did not answer.

"So who makes all this?" I said, my voice a little louder. "Most of it's handmade, isn't it?" I was growing angry. What was the matter, did they think I was being intrusive? Were they unable to stop and chat for a moment, for the sake of what most people call neighborliness?

"Quiché," Ernesto replied in a low voice, pulling a stack of frightful masks out of a box. "Guatemala. Indian, Indian," he added impatiently.

I could feel a prickling run across the lining of my brain, and my face got hot. I ambled down to my end of the hall, glancing back just in time to catch Ernesto's hard jade gaze following me. The man's eyes shifted, and he raised a cautious arm, more a gesture of defense or rebuff, it seemed to me, than a wave.

Thirteen days would pass before Ernesto bothered to pay a visit to my store: I counted them with a kind of sour satisfaction, growing every day more irritated by the briskness of their business, by the falseness of the laughter they used with their customers, by the overly open vowels of their mercantile bonhomie. In the meantime, I put aside my poetry — I had come to Taos to write, the bookstore merely a means to keep the wolf from the door — and began to read what few titles I had on Guatemala. Apparently the place was populated mostly by impoverished Indians and ruled by people of European and mixed blood — criollos and ladinos. I read one story about an Indian servant whose sole job was to get into the bed of his criollo master and warm it up for half an hour before the master retired, and another about ladino merchants who required young Indian slaves as loan collateral. Guatemala, it seemed, was a rather feudal place.

I poked my head out of my store between readings to observe the two criollos, or ladinos, or whatever they were, and their Indian. Archimedes' main job, in those first days, was to keep bringing load after load of goods on his back from the van — a name like that, I thought wryly, and they don't even allow him the leverage of a dolly. When once I beheld, astonished, Ernesto and Susana hunkered humbly beneath similar burdens, I decided it must be something of a show: they were trying to demonstrate solidarity with their Indian helper, for the gratified consumption of any egalitarian gringos who might be observing. But who did they think they were fooling? Not me!

The day Ernesto finally came in, I had been sitting at my desk, sipping Cuervo and trying to read a new title I had ordered: *I, Rigoberta,* the autobiography of the Nobel Peace Prize–winning Quiché Indian leader, Rigoberta Menchú. But my concentration was shot by my neighbors' trying to fob a plunky marimba off onto a loud and jolly Texan, and I slammed the book shut on the desk and watched the sunlit motes swirl madly, flashing like the synapses in my enraged mind. At last the Texan boomed hasta la vista, and a few minutes later Ernesto entered my store in his wary, lupine way, big nose twitching: sniffing around.

"Well, well! Ernesto! So how's tricks?"

He gave a crooked smile. "Tricks?"

I got up, upsetting my little dish of tequila salt, my head

thickly buzzing. "Yeah, how's business? Isn't that what you're all about?"

He peered at me with curiosity, then shrugged bonily and made a smoothing gesture with his hands. "You have to make money."

"Sure you do. The business of America is business! So why don't you do it right? Why don't you throw a grand opening? Kind of let folks in the community know you're here?"

"Is not necessary, I think," he said.

He was so sure of himself, and so dismissive of me!

"Well, Ernesto, you know what *I* think? I think you don't want to be a part of the community. I think yours is just another fly-by-night tourist operation into making a quick buck. That's what I think."

He regarded me with a patronizing, raised-eyebrow skepticism that infuriated me even more. I snatched the Menchú book and thrust it under his nose. "You're so wrapped up working for the Yankee dollar you probably don't even know what's going on in your own country. You should read this."

Ernesto didn't take the book. He just kept looking at me, the sneer trembling above his left canine. "You have read? Then you know much." And with that he walked out.

The Guatemalans, I noticed, fooled with their window display a lot, that window I had so conscientiously cleaned out for them that first day. They hung their jipijapa hats now here, now there, they draped their sashes this way and that over the little backstrap loom, they fiddled with the flutes. One bright morning as I arrived to open my store, I found Ernesto's lanky frame hunched in the window: he was trying to get a pair of gourd rattles to stand up against each other.

I knocked sharply on the glass in a taunting greeting, and he whirled to face me, kicking over the loom. He crouched there for a moment in a frozen lunge, like a creature — *Homo eco-*

nomicus var. *retailensis?* — in a museum diorama. I had to laugh. Later that day, as I kept picturing his startled face in the window, I got an idea.

I ordered nearly every title I could find on Guatemala and its strife. Then I emptied my window of its southwestern titles and filled it with these new ones: Payeras' *Days of the Jungle,* which described in hair-raising detail the beginning of the rural guerrilla movement in Guatemala; *Bitter Fruit,* an account of the United Fruit Company's and the CIA's depredations there; Amnesty International and Americas Watch reports documenting political disappearances and torture; more copies of the Menchú book. For good measure, I threw in Guillén's *Philosophy of the Urban Guerrilla,* Che Guevara's *Diary,* and Castro's *Collected Speeches.* For the backdrop, I hung posters of Sandino and Zapata, and, in the center, a giant one hailing Guatemala's Guerrilla Army of the Poor: fist with raised rifle, fiery red background, a total call to arms. Standing back after my labors were done, I was pleased to hear a passing tourist voice drawl, "Why, it's an ad for the goddamn revolution!"

Ernesto's anticipated second visit was not long in coming. He wandered in at about the time he normally went to the bank to make his daily deposit — he already had his blue bank bag with him, in fact, tucked tenderly into his waistband. He nodded gravely at me and began to peruse some of my new radical titles, prominently displayed on a table at the front of the store.

"You thought it was just window dressing, so to speak, didn't you?" I said with what I hoped was a galling joviality. "Well, you're wrong, señor. This is serious." I indicated, with a sweeping gesture, an entire bookcase of political titles.

Ernesto nodded again and continued to examine the new books, glancing up at me every now and then with a half-questioning expression. Something on the tip of his tongue; I predicted he was about to wheedle. Request, as politely as possible, that I tone things down. Say he agreed with a lot of this stuff, he really did, deep down, but that one had to be practical in this life. That this could not possibly be good for either of our businesses. That I knew as well as he how conservative were the times and the country we lived in, that the public would begin to think of our building as a Red center, to be avoided accordingly. And as I continued to smile smugly at him, the man was going to lose it. He was going to reveal his true colors, he was going to call it all garbage, subversion, he was going to froth at the mouth the way the ruling class of his country always frothed at the Communist Menace, and he was going to march his unglued self out in a tremendous huff.

But he didn't. All he did was flip through a couple more books, then glance with feigned surprise at his watch.

"Ah!" he said, tapping its face. "Bank!"

I was left smirking in the breeze of his departure. Bastard!

After a couple of weeks of seriously declining sales, I almost declared my point made and returned my bookstore to its former condition. But I stuck with it a little while longer, and that is when I noticed something fantastic beginning to happen: a completely new clientele was showing up regularly at my place. I hadn't known it before, but there existed in the area a fellowship of people with a deep and abiding interest in Latin American politics. They included committed artists and musicians from Taos and Santa Fe and the San Luis Valley in Colorado, graying La Raza militants from Las Vegas, Latin American Studies students from Albuquerque, and they were gradually appearing at my bookstore, not just to browse and buy but to meet each other and post flyers and converse with me about the state of the world. I felt a community in the making, and for the first time since arriving in Taos, I began to feel a real sense of usefulness and belonging. And with this new sense of things I let up on the booze. Alcohol, as one of my visitors said, was counterrevolutionary.

My hostility to the Dreyfuses, whom I now referred to as "those petty bourgeois elements down the hall," remained unabated, however, and I was delighted to learn that they were searching for another location for their shop. I envisioned, if I could somehow scrape the money together, taking over their space and converting it into some kind of people's coffeehouse.

It was also, I believed, my political and moral obligation to enlighten Archimedes about his situation, and about Guatemalan politics in general. Perhaps I could even succeed in luring him away from the Dreyfuses and into my budding new community. So one day, during the afternoon doldrums when the Dreyfuses were out looking at real estate, I went over to visit Archimedes. I found him sitting on a stack of fabric, staring off into space, his spidery fingers rapidly weaving a jipijapa hat. He smiled broadly at me, his fingers not missing a move. Though my Spanish was not good, and he was not much of a talker, he spoke cautiously and clearly, and I did manage to learn a few things about him. For one, he apparently hadn't known the Dreyfuses for long; he had hitched up with them in Los Angeles only a few days before they decided to come to Taos. For my purposes, this was good, as it suggested that he didn't owe them any particular loyalty. He also, as I had suspected, didn't seem to know much about the political situation in Guatemala, or at least wasn't letting on that he did. I invited him to come down to my bookstore, and as there were no customers at Cosas at the moment, he consented.

I showed him the Menchú book, and he studied her picture on the cover. I had read that a Guatemalan Indian can tell the very village where another is from from the patterns and colors of the other's clothing, and I contemplated him indulgently as he tried to so place her.

I attempted to tell him the Menchú story, about how her father had been burned alive by government soldiers, and how her brother and mother had been "disappeared" and tortured, just because they asked for their rights and because they were thought to associate with people the government believed to be communists. The government of Guatemala was extremely harsh with Indians suspected of association with the "sub-versives," I told him. Then I went on provide a vivid descrip-tion, miming where my Spanish failed me, of the many tortures reserved for enemies of the government, from the crude (I feigned blows to his solar plexus) to the sophisticated (I un-plugged a lamp and held the cord to my gums and crotch to show where the electric shocks were applied). There was the "ahogadito," or "little drowning," in which water, optionally spiked with chile or ammonia, is forced up the prisoner's nose. Then there was the "picana," or cattle prod, and the "caballito," in which the prisoner is made to straddle a narrow pole. I felt a twinge in my sinuses and a pang in my prostate as I told of these torments.

Archimedes listened anxiously to all this in a way that made me think he thought that *I* was somehow threatening him with these things. I tried to clarify what I was saying by showing him another book, in Spanish, on the subject, but from the way he looked at the words, I could tell he was illiterate. Instead, his eyes fastened on the logos of the many groups — trade unions, women's and students' organizations, guerrilla armies — that were opposed to the Guatemalan government. He turned the pages back and forth and studied those five-pointed stars, clasping hands, fists clutching AK-47s, sickles crossed by ma-chetes. I attempted to explain some things about these groups, but it was hopeless. We heard a customer clomp into Cosas, so he left me, a confused and frightened look on his face. I figured I'd better learn better Spanish before I attempted such an "edu-cation" again.

And speaking of learning Spanish, a few days after Archimedes' visit a man who looked exactly like my old Spanish teacher in high school, middle-aged and jowly, dressed impeccably in a gray silk suit, came into my bookstore. He browsed so intently that I was too intimidated to speak to him at first. Finally he turned to me, and in an exigent baritone demanded to know if

I was the owner of the store. I told him yes, and then he asked if it was "together" with the store down the hall.

"Oh, no, we're completely separate entities," I said. "Our businesses are very different. You see, they profit directly from exploitation, selling goods made by the poorest people of their country. I profit, when I profit at all, from books that in many cases expose that very exploitation."

The man glared at me in hard disbelief.

I watched him as he left. He paused at the Cosas display window, where Archimedes was arranging something. He spoke to him, and Archimedes crawled out of the space. The man placed his diamond-ringed hand on Archimedes' shoulder, and Archimedes went down the street with him. I thought it a little strange, but then shrugged it off as just another of the "Latino connections" my store would someday be famous for making.

A few days later, I again heard the man's baritone, rising to ever-more-demanding heights, echoing down the hall, counterpointed by Ernesto's nervously high objections. An American voice was telling them both to shut up. Something big was happening at Cosas. I hurried down to see.

The American whose voice I'd heard wore the green uniform of the INS, the immigration service, and there was another agent with him. The man in the suit stood with his ringed hand again on Archimedes' shoulder. Archimedes looked terrified. A fart of fear mingled with the copal incense.

Ernesto's long, pale fingers trembled as he handed some papers from his desk to the INS man, and his awkward elbow knocked over a basket of trouble dolls. The agent leafed through the documents, shaking his head mechanically.

The man in the silk suit grew impatient. "I have told you, this establishment is a front for the subversives," he insisted, glaring at me again.

He barked an order to Archimedes, and Archimedes pointed to a trunk.

"The propaganda is in there," the man told the agents. "That is where you will find their instructions."

The second agent opened the trunk. On top was Guatemalan clothing, bright with animal iconography. The agent took the clothing out, and at the bottom of the trunk were some yellowed newspapers adorned with some of the initials and logos I had shown Archimedes in the book.

"Terrorists," the man in the suit repeated. "They have links to the guerrillas. My government knows this."

"I don't know about that, sir," said the second agent.

The first agent kept looking over their documents, still shaking his head slowly. Ernesto's sallow face took on an even deeper waxiness, and his pink-rimmed eyelids began to flutter.

In another moment, the agents were patting him and Susana down and handcuffing them.

"Why?" cried Susana. "What for you do this?" Her jet eyes fastened on me accusingly.

By the time the agents had finished locking Ernesto and Susana in the cage of their vehicle, the man in the suit had Archimedes sequestered in his white car.

"To this one I give immunity," he said pompously, referring to Archimedes. The car had diplomatic plates.

One of the agents came back and locked up Cosas, and I was abandoned to the appalling silence.

It took me the rest of the afternoon to come to my senses and start calling human rights groups. I gave them as much information as I knew, hearing my voice distant and dead. They said they'd look into it.

I stayed close by the phone. A few days later a woman from one of the Catholic groups called back to say they had been unable to stop Ernesto and Susana's deportation.

"We couldn't get political amnesty for them even though we could prove that Ernesto, at least, had been arrested and tortured by the Guatemalan government on at least one previous occasion," she said wearily. "The problem is, the State Department insists that most Central Americans in the United States illegally are what it calls economic, rather than political, refugees. In other words, they're just up here to work, according to State. Normally the INS wouldn't send agents all the way to Taos just to bring in a couple of people, and the Dreyfuses probably knew that, but ironically, ever since Governor Anaya declared New Mexico sanctuary for Central American refugees, the feds have been doing these kinds of raids just to show who's boss. And that guy that came with them, the one with the car with the consular plates? We think we know who you're talking about; he works for the Guatemalan Consulate and he's bad news. He must have put a lot of pressure on the INS about the Dreyfuses. Unfortunately, if he's so convinced their store was some sort of 'front' for the guerrillas or whatever, he can make it real rough for them down there in Guatemala, too. You say you don't know what caused him to get suspicious about them?"

"No," I lied. "I don't."

I removed all the revolutionary literature from my window, and sooner rather than later, the Latinos and the political people stopped coming to my store. Perhaps they had heard about what had happened and rumors of my role in it. Who knows what kind of atrocious figure I had become in their eyes?

Meanwhile, I kept hoping against hope that Ernesto and Susana's disappearance would be a temporary thing, that one morning they would come trudging back in, foreheads straining against tumplines, backs heaped with gaudy bundles of new dream snakes, yarn paintings, grinning masks, that once again they would fling wide the doors of Cosas and I would have the chance to go down there and beg them to forgive my misunderstanding.

One late October day, as the clouds lay low and heavy over the Sangres de Cristo, I heard a van pull up outside, and my heart leaped. But the van had U.S. Government plates: it was from Customs. As the first snow of the season swirled, two men started clearing everything out of Cosas and into the van. For a while I watched them; and then I locked my door, shutting myself in my store. I poured myself a big one and drank. Outside, the snow came down. I poured myself another, and another. I leaned against my bookshelves and closed my eyes and succumbed to a phantasmagoria of lurid images: soldiers burning villages; miserable Indians in their bright costumes scattered on the steps of cathedrals, as drunk as I; people with their thumbs tied behind their backs being "disappeared" by death squads. I fell to the floor and soon felt the burning pain of my own vomit in my nose and throat: the "ahogadito."

Weeds

I was trying to stay clean, but it was tough. Sometimes I'd tie off and boot up blood, watch it swirl into the empty syringe. Then I'd slam it back home. Over and over. Play with it like that. Each time I slammed it, it gave me a rush. My limbs grew heavy and my bowels froze, as if they thought it was the real thing too.

I'd moved into a tiny studio apartment across town, away from my old haunts and connections: that was the first step. Now I needed something to get my mind off dope, keep me busy, wear me out. And I needed an income, since I was no longer dealing. So it was serendipity that led me to cross paths with McGrath at a downtown café.

I knew McGrath from my law school days, but hadn't seen him since I dropped out three years before. He was surprised to see me, asked me where I'd been. Sick, I said. A blood thing, like anemia. But I was all right now.

McGrath had become an attorney for the city. His murky brown tie matched his neat ponytail. I told him I was looking for a job.

"So you never got your J.D.?" he said in a quiet voice.

"Nope."

"Yeah, I remember you were pretty burned out on law. You were one of the radicals. What was it you used to say? '"Radical lawyer" is an oxymoron.'"

I didn't want to talk politics. I told McGrath I was looking, preferably, for a job outdoors, where I could breathe fresh air and get strong again.

"Go down to Parks and Rec," he said. "They're looking for someone to develop this community garden thing on the west side. Weren't you the guy who used to grow his own because you were against, how did you put it, corporate agriculture?"

He waited for me to take the bait, but I just stared out the window.

"Anyway, they want to turn this lot next to the new Trammell Crow building into a people's garden. It's an experimental thing. Pretty progressive, for Texas. The position's been listed for a while, so I guess there haven't been too many applicants. Hey, if you go for it, put me down as a reference."

I went to check out the site, and I could see why the job had remained unfilled. The ground was dry and pottery-hard, with only a few wild morning glories and goats' heads cracking its pale surface. Its ruts and oil stains suggested it had once been a parking area, perhaps for the machinery used to build the building McGrath had mentioned, which rose directly to the north, a big glass monolith that reflected the clouds like something out of a Magritte painting. The building, I later learned, had been built there to take advantage of the tax breaks given to those who participate in urban renewal. Apart from some warehouses further south and a housing project to the east, it was the only inhabited structure around.

I had to use the toilet, so I walked to the building, weaving my way through the two dozen or so cars huddled near the entrance. One of the cars, a forest-green Jaguar, sported an ironic vanity plate that read MENS REA — Latin for "guilty mind," as I remembered from law school. Revolving doors spun me into an icy foyer. A sour-faced guard behind a massive desk glared at me. To his right stood a gigantic, nightmarish bouquet on a marble table, and etched into the wall behind him was a gilt-lettered list of tenants, most of them law firms.

"Hep ye?" said the guard.

"No," I said. I spun myself out of the building. To hell with it. I'd piss behind my truck, and I did. Then I walked the lot again, trying to imagine it converted into a lush farm. I thought of those suited lawyers, trapped in their glass prison, gazing with envy at us free, half-naked peasants. I enjoyed the thought of their annoyance at the noise of our tillers and the sight of our messy compost piles and makeshift cold frames and ragged scarecrows, their disgust at the wafting odors of the fresh manure and blood meal and sewage sludge we dug into the soil.

I applied for the job, and I got it. It was a category 6 position, low-paying, but I went eagerly to work, put in ten-, twelve-hour days in the sticky spring heat. What I had to do was till the land and divide it into twenty-foot by twenty-foot plots, and hope gardeners would come to rent the plots. I was also to build a compost heap using materials from whomever I could get to donate. The gardeners had to provide their own seeds, tools, and fertilizers. No pesticides or herbicides allowed.

Parks and Rec, despite my entreaties, failed to send a plow to rip the soil, but they lent me a couple of rototillers, and the Texas Youth Commission sent a young Latino gangbanger to help with the tilling. He was putting in his community service hours for a drive-by shooting he'd been involved in.

"I didn't think they were gonna make me do no hard labor, bro," he said as I helped him wrestle his tiller out of the muddy hole it had dug itself into. A drop of sweat trickled down his temple and joined the teardrop tattoo at the corner of his eye.

"Oh, it's great," I said. "Good exercise. Fresh air. You'll sleep well tonight!"

"Shit. My parents spent their whole lives bustin' their ass in the fields. You think I wanna do the same?"

We leaned on the handlebars of our machines and wiped our brows. We gazed at the glass building. It looked cool, like a big ice cube.

A Cutlass Supreme lowrider cruised around the block. My gangbanger watched it.

"Catch you later, ése," he said. The sidelong look he gave me as he strode away warned me that he wouldn't much appreciate my snitching on his truancy. He talked to the men in the Cutlass. Then he climbed in with them, and they drove away.

Because his specialty was shooting people from moving cars and I could be found standing in a lonely open field all day, I took his unspoken warning somewhat seriously. And since I couldn't very well ask the authorities for another helper without betraying this one, I did the rest of the tilling myself, faithfully filling out his time cards. It was I who slept well at night, my arms and legs inert posts, my stomach muscles so sore I felt strapped to the bed by iron bands.

By late May I had the place plowed and divided into blocks. Each block contained four plots and a compost bin. The weeds grew fast all over, especially in Block G, which became infested with wild morning glory. Getting rid of the morning glory turned out to be an endless task, with every bit of chopped root springing into a vigorous life of its own. At one point I was tempted to break the rules of organic gardening and douse Block G with Roundup or Spike or some other brawny poison. But instead I cut a trench around it and hoped the willful weed would not spread beyond it.

I took it upon myself to flyer the nearby housing projects, and waited for takers. An elderly Chinese woman came along one morning, felt the soil, smelled it, said something I couldn't understand, and disappeared. A couple of Deadheads wandered by and asked if they could grow hemp there "for rope and cloth." No, I said, but what about flax or some other fiber crop? They left. A rural-looking family in an ancient pickup offered to take the whole site "off my hands."

At one point I solicited a group of young African Americans passing by on the street.

"Say what?"

"Yeah, look, I'll give you a plot for free for the season. Just try it, see if you like it."

The girl turned to the two boys. "You niggas want chop cotton?"

They all bent over in laughter.

"Y'all want chop cotton for free?" she asked them again, and they went through the same routine. I stood there with a shit-eating grin, wishing they'd just go away.

The paper ran a little feature on the project. But no one, apparently, was seriously interested in gardening there. Maybe my own little vegetable patch, which I'd put in near the street so everyone could see it, scared them away: the tomatoes were speckled with disease, the chard scalded by the sun, and the squash had some kind of worm that bored right into the heart of the plant.

The big main compost heap was growing fine, though, and I consoled myself by toiling long hours on it. Groundskeepers from a variety of buildings brought me bag after bag of grass clippings and leaves. One morning I received a big load of horse manure from the racetrack, piled high in a deuce-and-a-half truck, the driver joking that this was thoroughbred stuff, guaranteed to make plants grow real fast. I crumbled those road apples in my hand, admiring their rich brown color. I recalled reading in some gardening book that feces were brown because they consisted largely of spent blood cells, whose hemoglobin contained iron. Now this dead blood would turn into iron in the soil. And if someone would just come along and plant a garden with it, that iron would someday grow back into blood.

I dug a crater into the compost pile and spent most of that afternoon pitching the manure up into it. At the end of my labors, I climbed to the top of that manure-filled volcano and surveyed my lot. Knee-deep in horseshit, I looked out over its barrenness, at my own failed garden, at weed-filled Block G, at the lawyers' glass tower, at the gray housing projects from which the gardeners were presumably to come but didn't, and suddenly I was glad McGrath had yet to stop by and see how I was doing. I couldn't bear the possibility of his successful-lawyer's condescension, or the way he would surely wrinkle his nose at my stinking creation.

I felt my blood invaded by my old defeatism and depression. My connection always used to call smack "shit," and I thought I knew why. Smack was life and death, and it was all shit. I thought of those little pellets of black tar the size of mouse turds, how I'd dissolve them in the spoon and suck the juice up through the cotton and spike it, pull blood up into it and watch with fascination the way the blood swirled and mixed into the shit. Then I'd slam it all home, and that was life, and that was death, that blood and that shit.

I heard a vehicle at the garden gate and looked down to see a man drive up in a mud-spattered Toyota pickup. In its bed lay an oversized German shepherd amid an array of well-worn garden tools. I slid down the compost pile to meet them.

The dog growled at me without lifting its chin from the floor, one of those long, deep rumbles.

"Shut up, Milquetoast," said the man, and it did, but without removing from me its I'm-gonna-get-you-later eyes, whites ablaze.

The man's name was David Halliday. He wore a Puritan's narrow beard, which made the cheekbones stand out on his severe, rutted face. He dressed in a pair of faded, clean overalls, and when he spoke to me, he hooked his thumbs into their shoulder straps.

I gave him the grand tour of the place. I showed him the

morning glory in Block G, telling him I was hopeful it wouldn't spread.

"Morning glory," he said, rolling the words around slowly. "Far too poetic a name. I call it bindweed."

And, amazingly, he chose two contiguous plots right there, in Block G.

"I like the challenge," he explained.

He began clearing his land that same afternoon, starting in the most infested corner and working his way methodically to the center, digging down at least a foot and a half and placing every bit of morning glory in a neat pile of green leaf and crisp white root. Milquetoast lay in the shade of the pickup and watched him.

By sunset I was willing to risk Milquetoast's hostility and approach Halliday and admire his handiwork.

"Heck," I said, "the way you work, I bet you could handle a whole farm."

"I'll bet I could, too," he replied. Milquetoast sighed.

"So let me ask," I said, "why don't you? I mean, what brings you here? Not that it's not great to have you here, I mean."

"That's just it, Squire. You need me."

Squire, he called me.

"Why do I need you?" I was playing along.

"Well, you see," he said, plunging his shovel into the ground, "to have a successful garden, first you have to get order. That means weeding out the parasites. I drove by, saw this bindweed patch, and said to myself, that man sure needs help with the parasites. Now let me ask *you*: how'd you get into this?"

Something about his self-righteousness pricked awake my own long-dormant polemical side, and I gave him my best rap about community and dropping out of the System and how the gardens were a part of that. All that stuff I'd believed in before getting strung out, before I decided that the System had absorbed and co-opted everything, and that there was no out, except for the peace I could find in a needle.

Halliday looked at me sardonically. "Community? Let me clue you in on something, Squire. Your community isn't going anywhere until you get rid of the parasites." He waved his hoe at the blighted neighborhood around us. "Comb the vermin out of the body politic. Burn the leeches. Pull the weeds."

I didn't think I liked Halliday very much, and after that conversation I left him pretty much alone. Still, he was kind of right. I felt I did need him in some way. I needed him on the garden's side. And I needed him on my side: his stern presence made me concentrate on my work and forget my feelings of defeat, feelings that inevitably led me to thoughts about the comforts of dope. So while he battled the morning glory, I tended the compost pile with renewed energy, adding more to it, breaking up the matted grass clippings, turning it. According to the gardening books I'd checked out from the library, the compost would make the plants strong and help them fight off disease, would serve as a mulch to keep weeds down, and would help the ground retain water: nourishment and medicine for the soil.

One June Friday, a very warm afternoon (in Texas, you don't want to exhaust the word "hot" before the truly hot months arrive), as I was pitching a donation of moldy old pecan leaves and hulls onto the pile with my pitchfork, the fork sank into something soft and rubbery, and blood spurted onto me. I had found a few nasty things in donations before — yellowed condoms, a pair of enormous old underwear, a dried, flattened cat — but this was the worst yet. A thick rubber bag of blood. The blood's blackness crazed my cracked and blistered hands. I jogged to the work shed to wash them with disinfectant.

And that's when I saw them coming down the lane, the two street people, man and woman. Their gait was stooped but vaguely defiant in the loose swinging of the limbs. They both wore sagging jeans and faded T-shirts, the man's a black one that read, ASK ME WHAT I DID LAST NIGHT.

"Yes?" I said brusquely as I scrubbed hard with a Cloroxsoaked rag. They annoyed me, because they reminded me of myself not too long ago. And I was pissed at them, at all street people, because I was thinking that maybe the bag of blood had come from the pecan-shrouded plasma donor center down the road. Every morning, street people huddled in front of the center waiting for it to open so they could sell their blood. Sometimes they were hired to do menial tasks in and around the place, and perhaps one of them, drunk or high, had thrown bags of tainted blood in with the refuse from the grounds. Blood tainted with the AIDS virus, for example, or hepatitis. After all, a good many of those donors were intravenous drug users — I myself had donated, when I was strung out — and therefore at high risk for such diseases. Probably one of them had donated blood that upon subsequent screening was found to be tainted with a virus and discarded, only to end up in my compost heap.

They wanted to rent a garden plot; if they could, that is, said the one called Johnny in the way some street people have of expressing themselves, veering in the same breath from an almost aggressive assertiveness to a self-doubting humility. Rosey backed up his demand, or petition, with a look at once defiant and shy. They were waxy pale, as if the blood I had drained from the punctured bag had in turn been drained from their bodies. Which maybe it had.

"I've got just the one for you," I said. Out of sheer spite, I took them out and showed them the plots in G next to Halliday's, who wasn't there at the time.

"Got a lot of weeds," said Johnny.

"Oh, they're not too bad. You can get them out."

Johnny looked at me doubtfully.

"So what's a weed?" I said. "A weed is any plant growing where you don't want it to grow." I'd gotten that out of a textbook I'd picked up called *Weed Science*. "So maybe you want it to grow there. So then it's not a weed."

Now Johnny was looking at me slyly, as though I were pulling his leg. But Rosey looked pleased.

"I like that," she said. "Just a plant, but growing where nobody wants it to grow."

Johnny and Rosey paid for their plot in coins wrapped in two dirty blue bandannas.

"We wanna get back to the land," were Johnny's parting words.

"Got to get back to the land," said Rosey.

A few days after renting Johnny and Rosey their plot, I encountered Halliday on the road behind the work shed, rolling a wheelbarrow of compost to his garden. Halliday by now had strict rows of tomatoes and peppers and eggplants on his impeccable land, and a stalk of corn in each corner like a razor-leafed sentry. He came every day to check on his crops, and, wary of vandals or thieves, he sometimes left Milquetoast there at night, leashed to a pole.

"I see there are some new kids on the block," he said with a thin and chilly smile.

"Oh, right. A couple took G-3."

Fixing me with his glittery gaze, he said, "They're diseased, you know."

"What disease?" I said sharply.

"The disease of dissipation, Squire. Drugs. Alcohol."

"Maybe. So what? So maybe it'll be good for them to work a plot. Clean them out. Restore them to health."

"Don't bet on it. They're not going to work it. They're defeated. These are people vanquished by nature." He picked an aphid from the hair of his arm and peered into its tiny face before rubbing it into his coveralls. "First of all, they've succumbed to the dictates of the opiate receptors in their brains. And in doing so you can be sure they've shared needles and given each other the virus. Believe me, I know the look. These are people who don't even have the will to disinfect their needles. They've let a virus, a brainless strand of DNA in a shell of protein, defeat them. No, I don't think they're going to be clearing and maintaining any garden."

I thought of the blood that had gotten splashed on me. It would be ironic indeed if, after all those years on the needle, and sharing needles, I were to get the disease now. If it was true the blood came from the blood bank, I should sue it. Therein lay another irony for this law school dropout. I glanced over at the lawyers' building. Right, guys?

The days passed, and Johnny and Rosey didn't come back. I knew Halliday was spoiling for a fight with his neighbors from the way he stood glaring at their plot, sharpening the wicked little worn-down blade of his hoe with hard strokes of his file. I suspected he was just whiling away the time waiting for them to show.

And they finally did show, on one of those monumentally fine days when the sky's a shellacked eggshell blue, the morning air is still cool, the soil deliciously friable from the previous week's rains. I was contentedly hauling manure to Block G's compost bin. The sun was so bright and the air so clear that I imagined I could hear the low hum of a trillion photosynthetic electrons in Halliday's lush crops leaping neatly into their higher orbits.

Rosey and Johnny stood before their plot for a moment, contemplating it soberly. Then Rosey knelt down and began tenderly to arrange a morning glory's tendrils, spreading them out evenly from the crown. Johnny squatted and watched, scratching his stubbled cheek slowly.

Halliday, leaning on his hoe, blinked.

"Hey, let me tell you something," he said. "That's a weed."

Rosey and Johnny looked up at him, startled.

"It's pretty," said Rosey.

And so it was, with its little trumpets of white, some of them marbled in a delicate pink, turned in unison to the sun.

"It's still a weed," said Halliday.

"It don't matter," said Rosey, spreading a tendril onto a bare patch of soil.

"Yes, it *does* matter." Halliday glanced at me. "You can't let your plot go to weeds. It's in the bylaws."

Technically he was right; the rules said you couldn't let your garden go to pot or you would forfeit your right to keep a plot. But I was the one who had rented them this already weed-infested ground, and now I felt it would be unfair to red-tag them. So I ignored the dispute, which Halliday, I'm sure, saw as a sign of cowardice.

"It's our plot," said Johnny.

"No, it's not *your* plot," said Halliday. "These are called the *community* gardens and you're not allowed to spread your weeds around. Hey, Squire," he called to me. "Tell these people about your community. Tell them how it's gotta be in the Revolution."

"This dude's bummin' me out," said Rosey, rising. "I can't take this scene."

She ambled down the driveway. Johnny gave Halliday a murderous look and caught up with her, and they wandered off in the direction of town.

Halliday chopped viciously at his soil. "Good-for-nothing sorry trash," he said. "The flotsam your Revolution loves and bleeds for. At least until your side wins. After that, it's off with their heads. As well it should be. Am I right, Squire, or am I right?"

I knew I should have stopped Halliday from invading their plot and clearing their land, but I didn't. By the next afternoon, their ground was clear and smooth as a billiard table. Then he did the same to the plot next to it, so that the entire block was immaculately, utterly weed-free. And he made sure it stayed that way.

Rosey showed up alone about three weeks later, trudging

down the road more stooped and gangling than ever. She paused to admire something on the ground and then proceeded to her plot.

"Say, Rosey?" I said, coming up behind her. "Rosey, I've decided to give you guys another plot. Where the soil's better?"

She smiled a sad, crooked smile. "Oh, no. I've got to tend Johnny and my's flowers."

She ambled on. When she got there she stopped, nonplussed, and contemplated her barren soil. She circled the whole block, as if that would give some explanation or perspective on what had happened. She avoided looking directly at Halliday.

Finally she turned to him and spoke, her head protruding turtlelike from her hunched shoulders. "What happened to my flowers?"

"Your *what*?" He was smiling his thin smile, and stood ramrod-straight beside his spading fork like the farmer in the painting *American Gothic*.

"My flowers. Somebody came on my land and killed all my flowers."

"Your *flowers*?" Halliday gave a snicker of contempt as he caught my eye.

"Uh, Rosey —" I said helplessly.

"What would you say," Halliday said, "if I told you I had taken out your flowers?" He stabbed his fork into the ground.

She stared at him. Then, in a wet, trembling voice, she said, "I'd say you got no right. You got no right."

"You bet I have a right," Halliday said, his own voice taut with rage. "I have a God-given right to clear out filth whenever and wherever I see it. Rid this land of filth, weeds, vermin, disease, and the things that spread them. Like you, and that fellow with you."

"Johnny?" she cried, jerking up straight, her eyes full of tinypupiled fury. "Johnny never did nothing to hurt you. You up-tight son of a bitch." She picked up a lump of manure and hurled it at him.

Halliday pulled his fork out of the ground and pointed the tines at her, the thin grin splitting his face. Milquetoast, roped to the pole, lunged forward with a snarl.

"All right, now," I said.

She whirled to me. "He got no right," she said, her voice a babble of grief. "Them plants weren't weeds. They were just plants growing in the wrong place. You said it yourself. I wanted them. *We* wanted them there. Now Johnny's dead."

She turned back to Halliday. "He wasn't filth, you mother-fucker. He wasn't no vermin." She approached him in a crouch. He crouched too, jabbing little thrusts at her, still grin-ning maniacally. They circled each other. She grabbed the tines. Milquetoast went berserk.

"All right, now, all right," I said, and grabbed the fork in the middle. We spun around in a crazy dance, each trying to wrest the fork from the other. In the background loomed the lawyers' building, big and solid and glacially reflective, and I couldn't help thinking two simultaneous, contradictory thoughts: What the fuck are you people looking at? and Well, aren't any of you going to come out and help me?

Eloy

There was a hill behind Santa Fe Voc Tech where Rudy, Eloy, and Severino would go to cut class and smoke. Rudy claimed he could see the pinta, the state penitentiary, from there. He said he could make out two guard towers and glints from the razor-wire fence. Severino drew his rubbery face into a squint and looked out beyond the tract housing and said he couldn't see anything. Eloy said he thought he could make out something on the tawny plain below the black mountains.

One freezing February morning Rudy pointed to what he said was smoke rising from the penitentiary. He said he could smell it, and that it smelled bad. "There some bad shit going down over there. It's a badass riot."

"It's like racial gangas fighting, ¿que no?" said Eloy.

"Or they were trying to escape," suggested Severino.

"Not even, bro," said Rudy darkly. "That's bros wasting bros."

Rudy knew a lot about the joint. He had an older brother in

maximum, cellblock 5, and an uncle who was a guard. Mr. Grimes, the chingón pelón bald bastard history teacher, liked to tell, when he was pissed at the class, the story of how Santa Fe County had turned down the chance to become the site of the University of New Mexico in favor of becoming that of the penitentiary. "The reasoning was quite simple," he said. "It was so your families would have you close to home."

"What an asshole, huh," Rudy said about Mr. Grimes. Eloy watched for him to flick his cigarette butt onto the orange gravel of their hill. Rudy had a bitchin bad way of flicking a butt off his thumb. He dressed like a cholo, with white T-shirt and baggy black chinos and a net over his hair. He had a wispy moustache that was going to look cómo que bad in a couple of years. Eloy dressed like Rudy, but he didn't have the face. Eloy's face was round and hairless and shiny brown-red: a face like a pinche apache, Eloy thought.

Severino shrugged. "You got two in the pinta, bro. How many you got at college?"

"Fuck you, homes," said Rudy, flicking the butt at Severino.

Severino was a real poor bro from the sticks south of town. His father was a mejicano wood man who sold piñón and cedar. Rudy sometimes called Severino abuelita, granny, and sometimes he called him mojao, wetback. He was an abuelita because he was careful, like an old lady, and he was a mojao because he was born in Mexico. A lot of the cholos hassled Sevvy because he was a mojao. He dressed like one — always jeans and a plaid cowboy shirt and cowboy boots with metal tips — and those cholos thought he was a real bumpkin and they were better than he. But Rudy's older brothers had been Brown Berets and had given Rudy a powerful sense of raza. Rudy would defend Severino to the death.

"Hey, you boys," boomed a voice behind them as they watched the smoke rise from the penitentiary. It was Mr. Gurulé. Nobody knew what he was, officially. Rudy said he was a rent-a-pig, but Sevvy said he was more than that, like maybe

a second vice principal. Whatever he was, he was always every-
where, rounding up truants. He was proud of his name, which
he said was both Spanish and French, but that didn't keep
people from calling him Gorilla.

Gorilla clapped his hands. "Let's go to class, carnales!" Gorilla was good cop/bad cop in one. Sometimes he was like a
big old bro; other times he was a real pinche chota. One night
he came to a pachanga at Rudy's party house way out on Agua
Fría. He pounded on the door: "Police! Open up!" And they did,
thinking it was a vacilada, a joke, and he laughed and came in
and drank a beer and ignored the weed. He was a weird dude.
But as Rudy said, a pig is a pig is a pig.

Gorilla hustled down the hill hungrily, hunting for more truants. Severino crushed his butt with the metal tip of his boot
and made a start to leave.

"Be cool, bro," said Rudy, stopping Sevvy with a hand on his
shoulder. "We're not pollitos to scatter when a gorilla comes
snorting around." They all laughed, but Eloy could tell Sevvy
was anxious to go. He didn't like to miss class too much.

Rudy came to the cafeteria one day soon after the prison riot
with a special fork that his uncle the guard had given him. It
was one of the new prison mess-hall forks that broke away
when you tried to stab somebody with it. At lunch Rudy
whipped it out and tried it on Severino. Severino jumped back,
spilling his milk. The tines of the fork stayed stuck in his coat.
Everybody laughed, including some jocks in Conquistador letters at the next table. When Severino sat back down, Rudy said
in a loud voice that one dead faggot at the joint had been found
with a baseball bat up his ass. "Fat end or skinny end?" said
Eloy, also loudly. The jocks stopped laughing and looked at
each other and at their plates, making signals with their eyes.
That's when Gorilla came over and asked to see the fork. He
looked at it and said ooh and ahh and qué suave. The jocks

split. After lunch Gorilla took Rudy and his fork to Mr. Weeks's biology class and Rudy got put through a show-and-tell.

Severino told Eloy about Rudy's show-and-tell. Severino was the only raza in Mr. Weeks's class: that class was on the preppie track, and nearly all preppies were Anglos. You had to have especially good grades to get into those classes, and you had to sign up for them special. Severino told how Gorilla made Rudy rush at him with the fork. The fork broke away and Gorilla pretended to be surprised and pissed and got Rudy in a half nelson and walked him around the room. Then Gorilla showed the class other weak spots on the body, using Rudy as a dummy: the soft spot behind the ears, the kidneys, the bridge of the nose. He saved the best for last: he drew his knee up into Rudy's crotch, hard enough to make Rudy bring his knees together and grab his huevos. A couple in the class snickered. Mr. Weeks grinned kind of sickly.

Rudy wanted to know which ones had laughed, but Severino said he didn't know. For sure Rudy wanted to waste Gorilla. He wanted to take out Gorilla's menudo with his blade and chop off his huevos and stuff them in his mouth. "I don't care if he *is* raza," he said.

Rudy's blade was a Super Automatic. It went straight out and in, like a snake's tongue. A cousin of Severino's had brought it up from Mexico at a time when Severino was being mad-dogged to the max by some cholos. Severino gave the blade to Rudy, and Rudy flashed it at the cholos and that was the end of the hassle. Now Rudy homestyled his moves on the hill, showing Sevvy and Eloy the quick slices he would make in Gorilla's big belly to take the menudo out. One day he was homestyling when Gorilla showed. Now was his chance, but he flicked the blade back in and shoved his hands in his pockets. Gorilla didn't say anything when he passed by, but he gave a wink and a thumbs-up to Sevvy. Sevvy gave two up back.

"You fucking signing the pigs now, ése?" said Eloy.

"He did it to me," said Severino.

"And you do it back, hey," Eloy said, and spat. "Lambiche, mamón."

Rudy got popped on the Fourth of July. He knocked over the Taco Hell with some older vato loco that neither Eloy nor Severino knew. Rudy and the vato chose the Fourth because people spent a lot of money that day on fast food to take to the fireworks and because most of the chotas were at the fireworks, keeping order. But there happened to be three plainclothes chotas in the Taco Hell parking lot watching the fireworks from there and the mojao dishwasher ran out the back and told them what was coming down. When the chotas busted into the Taco Hell Rudy held the Super Automatic up to the cashier chick's neck, but only for half a second, and then he put the blade down and surrendered.

Rudy told Eloy and Severino about how the biggest fireworks were saved for when he and the other bro were being led out of the Taco Hell in handcuffs and put in the chotamobile. It was like all of the fucking United States of Gringolandia was celebrating their bust. The chotas dropped the assault charge because Rudy had held the blade only for a second to the cashier chick's neck. Rudy had known that his shit was up, that he should give up then. He was smart.

"Gorilla asked me why I did it, and I said, chale, I figure I got two choices when I graduate, to work in one of those places or rob one. And why wait to graduation, right?"

Rudy was styling big, but he was bummed about the mojao dishwasher. The dishwasher, as it turned out, was a cousin of Severino's cousin, which meant he was Severino's cousin too.

"Fucking mojaos, man, snitching to the chotas to score brownie points," said Rudy.

"You should have let us in on it, bro," said Severino in a hurt voice. "Then I could have told my cousin to be cool."

"Let you in, you fucking abuelita?" Eloy said. "So you could

snitch before it even came down? You mojaos are all abuelitas."
Now Eloy sounded like those cholos who were always hassling
Sevvy.

Rudy was sent to the Boys' School in Springer, and Eloy didn't
see much of Severino the rest of the summer. Mostly Eloy
hung out at home, where his mother hassled him about being
friends with Rudy. Eloy lived alone with his mother; his father
was dead, his brothers in the armed forces. She didn't hassle
him directly, she would just look at him and say, "Ay hijo, ay,
m'hijo," and she bought a new rosary with big red beads. The
little house was always full of steam because she was always
boiling posole or beans. She would stand in front of the stove
and poke sadly at the pigs' knuckles in the pot, and Eloy knew
she was thinking about him. When he couldn't stand it anymore he went to the old spot behind Voc Tech to smoke. There
was a new anthill of red ants near the big piñón, built over the
summer. He thought he should take some of the little orange
rocks on top of the anthill for his mother's collection. She still
collected these piedritas de hormiga for healing and luck, a few
from each hill, even though Father Romero had told her it was
wrong. She said all the anthills were connected deep under-
ground and that these rocks, the ones on the very top, came
from a common place deep in the middle.

Down below on the plain they were rebuilding the pen.
Trucks moved on the highway, silently as the ants, carrying
things. A blue steel crane moved stiffly. The Sandía Mountains
behind were sharp but broken off at the end, like the broken
blade of a knife. Hidden behind the Sandías was Albuquerque,
a real city. Eloy watched the red ants toiling, and then put his
cigarette out in the hole on top of their hill. An ant crackled
under the coal, and the others began to swarm around crazily.
Even the ones far from the action quickly realized something
was fucked, and they began to rush around too, looking for the
enemy. Eloy remembered something Severino had told him

and Rudy in the old days, something he had learned in one of his classes, about how if we lived in a totally flat world, like drawings on paper, and then something came down on that paper, like a burning cigarette, we wouldn't know what the fuck was happening, we'd just see this hole burning wider and wider on our paper. That was because the cigarette was coming from a dimension we didn't know about. "Well," Sevvy went on, "we're not flat, so we can see things coming down on us, but how many dimensions might there be that we don't know about, how many things happening to us that we can't see?" Rudy had laughed in that way he laughed at Sevvy's shit, with a spontaneous spray of spit, and said, "Flat, huh, bro? I'm gonna stomp you flat, joto."

Watching the ants, Eloy thought he knew what Sevvy was talking about. These animals didn't know where the fuck that cigarette had come from. They might not have known where it came from, but they hung together, they defended their turf against whatever it was, just like a ganga. He picked out a few of the orange and pink pebbles and put them in his pocket for his ma.

"Check this out," he said, and kicked the mound until it was all fucked up.

Eloy found Severino at the gym on registration day, signing up for his preppie classes: Mr. Rodriguez's English class, Weeks's special science class. Sevvy was like a fish, a brown trucha, swimming flexibly among the gabachos. He was breathing anxiously through the pursed hole in his blubbery jeta-lips.

"What's happening, bro," said Eloy.

"Not too much, man. Heard anything from Rudy?"

Eloy said he hadn't.

"Fucking bummer, man." That's all Severino had to say about Rudy anymore.

"What's the bummer, bro?" Eloy shrugged. "He got popped,

that's part of the overhead." That's what Rudy called it, over-head.

Then he asked Severino: "You got a job this year, bro?"

"I just got this internship," said Severino. "It's sort of like a job."

"What's the pay?" Eloy rubbed the tips of his fingers to-gether.

"They don't really pay."

"They don't pay you shit *nothing?*"

"It's an internship. You just learn shit."

Sevvy was always doing this shit. Last year he was a page at the state legislature, and a legislator had once asked him in the rest room if he would let him suck his verguita. That was at the time of the riot, and the legislators were all excited about all the stories about the rapes and killings and shit. Sevvy said he didn't let him, but Eloy didn't believe him, he probably sucked the guy's too, the mamón.

"So where is this inter-whatever?"

"Internship. It's in the D.A.'s office."

Eloy took this in. "That's the pigs, bro."

"It's not the pigs," Severino objected. "It's lawyers."

"It's the lawyers for the pigs," said Eloy, turning away.

Eloy saw Sevvy only in passing over the next month. Sevvy wasn't dressing like a mojao anymore; now he dressed like a joto gabacho, in Docksiders and a sweater with the sleeves tied around his neck. He was going out with this gabacha chick. Sevvy introduced him to the chick, whose name was Ellen. She had pale blue lines for lips. Severino's big rubbery dark indio lips and the gringa with her pale no-lips, how did they suck face? Her long hair was like cornsilk and completely flat, and her eyes were blue as the dondiego flowers that Eloy's mother planted along the fence. She looked at Eloy with a kind of curi-osity. Eloy had on his dark wraparounds and she couldn't see his eyes, and he kept his face taut and expressionless, like a stone.

One morning in October Severino showed up at the hill. Eloy grunted a greeting. Severino asked for a smoke and Eloy gave him a Camel. They smoked in silence until Sevvy took something from his pocket.

"Check it out," he said.

It was the Super Automatic.

"I copped it from the juvenile probation officer's desk. He was keeping it as a souvenir."

Eloy checked it out. It still worked good. He put it in his pocket.

"Hey," said Sevvy, "that's Rudy's."

"What are you gonna do, homie, take it up to Springer to him?"

"I'm keeping it for him. It's Rudy's."

Eloy had his thumb on the button. The button had ridges. The thumb couldn't slip.

"*I'm* keeping it for him," he said.

Sevvy's dark lips began to tremble. "It's Rudy's, it's Rudy's."

"Don't worry, little abuelita," laughed Eloy. "I'll protect you from the cholos."

Severino was right, though: it was Rudy's shank. So Eloy didn't flash it as if it was his. He only flashed it once, to some wanna-bes. Wanna-be wanna-bes, Rudy always called them, because in Santa Fe there were no gangas or clickas to even wanna-be a part of. Eloy thought maybe he could form them into a clicka and have it ready and waiting for Rudy to take over when he got out of Springer. He flashed Rudy's shank and the wanna-bes saw it, but nothing happened.

Severino's gabacha chick walked up to Eloy in the high school parking lot.

"Eloy, we gotta talk." Her eyes were big and round and blue.

"Let's go," said Eloy, looking over her shoulder at her car. She drove a purple Karmann Ghia.

"I've gotta go to class," she said. "But meet me after. Downstairs in E."

Eloy chilled by himself behind the library, toking a juby. He wondered if the chick wasn't coming on to him. She liked raza, otherwise she wouldn't be going with Severino. Maybe she liked to help raza, the way Anglos like to help stray dogs. Maybe she had already helped Sevvy enough, and now wanted to help him. Maybe he turned her on.

He hung around the hallway of E building. He was surprised to see Severino come out of one of the classrooms dressed in nothing but a sheet. Sevvy started pacing, muttering to himself.

"Bro," said Eloy. He wanted to laugh.

Severino looked up and turned darker. "This tacuche's a toga," he explained. "We're rehearsing for a play."

"What play?"

"*Oedipus Rex.*"

"Ate a puss?"

Severino gave a little laugh. "Not even. *Oedipus.* A Greek tragedy. This guy screws his jefa, his mom, and then punches out his eyes. I gotta go back in, check you out later."

Sevvy was a fucking loco locochón. There weren't plays like that, not in high school. It was probably about a dog that chased cats. Rex was the dog.

Ellen was the first to come out of the classroom when the period was over.

"Let's go," she said to Eloy. "I don't want Sevvy to see us."

So she did have something in mind, Eloy thought. He led her to the hill. There was no one in sight, not even on the football field below. The October sky was dark blue and the orange gravel on the anthill glittered.

"Did you know that half of the guys at Springer end up down there at the penitentiary?" she said. She was smoking, elbow propped on her crossed left arm, her long blond hair in the breeze. She looked like a chick in a movie.

"So what?" said Eloy. He knew his eyes were looking at her quiet and half-lidded, like a horny toad's.

"Severino doesn't really need anybody to protect him or anything, you know," she said, without taking her own gaze off the view.

"Because he's with you now, huh. You buy him all the clothes, ¿que no?"

She didn't say anything for a while. Then she said, "Sevvy really wasn't going to give the knife to Rudy. He just wanted to prove to you guys that he had the, you know, that he was brave enough to swipe it. Then he was going to get rid of it. He could get into a lot of trouble if it's found."

Eloy had his hand deep in the pocket of his black chinos, his thumbnail clicking across the ridges of the Super Automatic's button. She was going to ask him to give it to her, he knew that. There would be many different ways of giving it to her. He could give it to her right in the neck, the way Rudy had done with the cashier chick at the Taco Hell, and fuck her right here. He might get sent to Springer for it, but so what, that's where Rudy was, and though maybe Rudy would be pissed because he fucked Severino's gabacha chick, maybe not. Or he could hand it to her gently, nicely, and maybe sometime after that she would go with him on walks on the east side of town, where the Anglos' adobes huddled cozily in the snow. Or he could just stick the blade in the piñón and snap it off, showing her he didn't give a shit. Or he could bury it deep in the anthill, and it would stay there, their secret. There were many choices. We had lots of choices in life, Gorilla liked to say. Eloy's thumbnail went up and down the ridges, counting them.

"Well, you think about it, Eloy," she said after a long silence. "I gotta get back and rehearse for the play."

"Hey," said Eloy, "is that true it's about this guy and his, you know, his mom?"

"The play? Yeah, but first he kills his father. But he doesn't know it's his father. And he doesn't know it's his mom until later, either. When he finds out, he puts out his eyes. Then she commits suicide. It's like this really dysfunctional family."

Eloy clicked his nail along the ridges of the Super Automatic. "That's fucked, man. That's cómo que fucked. There's some bad shit that comes down all over, ¿que no?"

"There sure is."

Dogs

Behind the Bermúdezes' red-tiled house outside of San Salvador, at the edge of their coffee plantation, gaped a large, smoldering rubbish pit dug into the black volcanic soil. Everything was dumped in the pit: cankered coffee berries, kitchen scraps, spent shell casings. Douglas Bermúdez once saw there what looked to be a swatch of human hair on a patch of scalp.

Sometimes curs would get trapped in the pit and couldn't get out, and Douglas's father, a captain in the Guardia Nacional, would shoot them. A bitch with a bone-tipped tail like a rattlesnake's once whelped there: Douglas watched the pups come out, wriggling wet and red. The captain drew his sidearm and handed it to Douglas and told him to shoot. Douglas wept. "Shoot, faggot," said his father. The gun trembled in Douglas's hand. The father snatched the 9 mm and got off one round before it jammed. The wounded dog yelped as pups kept coming blindly out of her.

A teenage girl was seen scavenging shell casings there in the dry season. They said she was getting them for the guerrillas to reload. A soldier threw a discolored grenade in the pit like a little rotten pineapple, killing her and a naked child standing at the edge. After this, the captain had the pit bulldozed over.

The American nuns were buried in a pit, too. Douglas understood that his father had shown the American investigators where they were buried, and that is why he and his father and mother had to change their names and leave the country. Douglas Bermúdez was now Max Ponce. He was twelve, and he and his parents now lived in Texas.

Max Ponce sat in pajamas in a leather armchair, cradling his father's 9-mm semiautomatic in his lap. He watched two dogs prance proud but bewildered up and down the deserted street of the half-built Texas development. They were two miniature Lassie dogs with long honey-and-white coats and fine, elegant snouts. They pranced down the cul-de-sac, made the circle, and pranced back. Max tucked his knees under his chin and took careful aim at the dogs.

The two little Lassies pranced away again, daintily. Max massaged the worn grip of the gun against the black bristles above his ear. His hair was military short, the way his father liked it.

Max relaxed his legs and slipped his hand into the gaping fly of his pajamas. He ran the muzzle of the gun through his pubic hair. The pubic hair was long. His genitals were inflamed from masturbation, and he pressed the cool gunmetal against them. He thought of the naked women he had spied on that day at the lake and grew excited again; and then he thought of the picture in the newspaper of the naked bodies of the raped nuns hauled up from the pit and grew ashamed. He pressed the muzzle into his balls until they hurt with the deep pain of balls. He rocked in his chair and pressed. Then he picked up the phone and tried to call Father Ortiz at the parish. There was no answer. So he called the sheriff's department.

*

Donna, the dispatcher, referred the call to Deputy Epimenio "Eppy" González, who spoke Spanish. Eppy thought the Ponce boy sounded awfully distraught just to be reporting something as trivial as two loose dogs in a quiet suburb.

"Whose dogs are they, do you know?" he asked. "Calm down, son."

"I just don't want them to get hurt." And the boy hung up.

Epimenio stretched, and thought about the Ponce family. The sheriff's department had begun getting calls from worried neighbors about the Ponces soon after they moved to the Northgate development. Who were they? the callers, housewives, wanted to know. Where did they come from? Spanish-looking men in Jeep Cherokees arrived to visit the Ponces at any hour of the night, they said. One was a military man, in full dress uniform!

Sheriff MacPherson told his deputies to tell folks that Mr. Ponce was a Mexican businessman. And that Mexican businessmen are sociable people. Mi casa es su casa and all that good stuff. The Northgate folks should welcome them to the neighborhood. Go drop in on their new neighbors from south of the border and say hello!

More recently, a Northgate lady had called to report that the little Ponce boy, Max, played hooky from school. He hid down by the lake and spied on the nudists. He shouldn't be doing that, she said. There shouldn't *be* a nudist beach in the first place, but she didn't want to beat that dead horse. That's what they got for living so close to Austin, the Sodom and Gomorrah of Texas, she knew that. But the sheriff's people should patrol down there more often. Children shouldn't be there, playing hooky.

But Sheriff MacPherson told his deputies that Max's father, enraged over some kind of teasing his son had endured at the school, had withdrawn the boy from classes. And that was just all right, the sheriff said. He told his deputies to ignore calls about the boy playing hooky, even if he was down at the lake all day spying on the nekkidies. Just leave that family be, said the sheriff. Let them get adjusted to their new country at their own speed.

Epimenio sighed, leaned back in his swivel chair and felt a needle of pain in the small of his back. Lord, maybe another kidney stone. A month ago one had knocked him down flat on the floor of the station, the pain shooting through his back, his abdomen, the insides of his thighs. The doctor told him it was a disease of middle age. He would probably need an operation. Epimenio didn't like the idea of middle age; didn't like the word, which meant nothing other than getting old.

There was another word the doctor used that bothered him just as much: "sedentary." The doctor had asked if his lifestyle wasn't pretty sedentary. "Do you sit in one place a lot?" he wanted to know. "Well, I sit a lot in three places — " said the deputy, "my office chair, my Barcalounger at home, and the driver's seat of my patrol car. Humble ain't the liveliest county in Texas, you know, doc; the law ain't exactly kept on its toes in these parts." "That's a fact," said the doctor. "Well," Epimenio said on leaving, "at least it's not hemorrhoids," and they laughed.

Least of all did Epimenio like the idea of an operation. So he secretly visited doña Eufemia, the ancient Mexican curandera. She gave him a mixture of foul-smelling herbs and instructed him to drink their "infusions." He promptly felt a grittiness in his urine and then had passed a stone, the pain of it excruciating every millimeter of the way. A torture of nature worse than any man could invent. He had a bag of the herbs in his desk drawer, but had never yet made the tea there at the station. He didn't want to put up with the ribbing. But now he brought out the little plastic bag and a bottle of Tylenol from his drawer and headed for the kitchen. What the hell. So he was middle-aged. So he had kidney stones. So a Mexican witch doctor's tea happened to work.

Donna was in the station's kitchen, standing by the big Braun coffeemaker, as if waiting for him. Her birdlike black eyes — she was part Pawnee — didn't miss the bag of herbs in his hand.

"Gonna roll you one?" she said.

Epimenio explained to her the story behind the herbs. No point in trying to hide anything from Donna. But she hung around even after he told her all about his kidney stones. He was sure she was waiting to hear about the Ponce boy. For a lowly dispatcher, she was a busybody. But as the saying went in these parts, I may be humble, but then this is Humble. Meaning even the most menial person had a right to know. Donna wasn't a meddler, but she had a need to know. She should have been a detective.

"He hung up on me," said Epimenio, pouring boiling water through the strainer.

"Hmm," she said, turning down the corners of her fat-hidden mouth. "It stinks."

He didn't know whether she meant the herbs or the whole strange situation with the Ponce boy and his family.

"You think I should go talk to him, don't you?" Epimenio said.

"Hey, I want you to stay here and talk to *me,* hon." It was coffee-time banter, but what she meant was yes, she thought he should talk to the boy. He knew she wanted him to take advantage of this window the boy's call had opened, and take his sedentary self out to Northgate and find out about that peculiar family once and for all. She was not satisfied with what she knew of the Ponces. Nobody at the department was, except maybe Sheriff MacPherson, who seemed to know a few things about them that nobody else did.

"I'll clue you," Donna said. "They say the Freddies are behind those folks. What I say, anyway."

Epimenio drank a sip of the acrid tea and felt his stomach turn. Donna, like most people in Humble, was suspicious of the federal government. They thought of it as something remote and evil. They seemed to forget that LBJ, native son of these parts, was once the head of it. Epimenio thought LBJ was one of the greatest presidents, Vietnam aside. He was great on civil rights. Before LBJ, nobody with a name like Epimenio González could have become a deputy in Humble County. So Epimenio didn't feel the same aversion toward the feds as most folks did, though he didn't say so. If the feds were somehow involved with the Ponces, as Donna suggested, then it was none of his business. On the other hand, he was the only law enforcement officer in Humble who spoke Spanish, and he had gotten a call from a Spanish-speaker, so it was his duty to investigate it. He could call the boy back, handle it over the phone, but that would be sedentary.

"I'm going out there," he said, squinting his eye against the tea's vapors.

Max hated his new American school. He hated his peers, those oafish, red-faced bully boys and the equally brutish, ruddy-kneed girls. They delighted in surrounding him in a circle and asking him what his father did. "Coffee business," he was forced to say every time, because this was what his father had instructed him to say. This provoked great merriment among the children, who mimicked his accent and said his dad must be that dorky greaser Juan Valdez in the coffee ad. They soon hit on Maxwell House as a permanent nickname. A teacher once overheard them in class discussing what roast he was — dark or medium — and the teacher himself seemed to be re-pressing his amusement. Tears burned Max's eyes. After class the teacher held Max back and gave him an angry explanation: "You know what 'to roast' means, Max? It means to tease. They're just teasing. Lighten up, Max."

Max always slipped off the school grounds at noon to eat lunch by himself. One foggy day Billy and his followers Jason and Cody tailed Max and sneaked up on him as he sat beneath a live oak. They inspected his food, and said it was okay. A ham sandwich — they had expected a burrito or a taco. So maybe he wasn't such a spic after all, said Billy. Maybe he was just real tan. A lot of sunshine where you're from, huh, Maxwell? Maybe your ass is white. Let's see your ass.

He struggled, but they got his pants down. You're roasty brown all over, Maxwell House! Maybe you lie nekkid in the sun with the queers down by the lake. Maybe you're queer, Maxwell!

They left him sobbing under the oak. He longed to tell them all who his father really was, a captain in the Guardia. He longed to take his father's 9 mm to school and show them how he could shoot them all like dogs in a pit.

Napoleón Ponce, formerly Captain Diógenes Bermúdez, and his wife, Cecilia, Max's mother, cruised up I-35, returning home to Northgate from a shopping spree in Austin.

"I hope he's all right," she said. "We shouldn't have left him alone all day."

"Mami mima mima Mami," said the captain. "You worry about him too much, so that's why he's the way he is. He didn't want to go, so what could we do?"

The Lincoln's suspension was dreamy, the curves of the highway fluid. One thing you could say about the gringos, the captain often said, was that, like the ancient Romans, they built fine chariots and excellent roads.

"It's his age," said Cecilia. "Twelve is a hard age for any child, especially one so uprooted."

"Everything's timing, as the gringos say," the captain said blandly, though he could feel the rage bulk in him.

Yes, with Max the timing had always been off, he thought. Even Max's real name, Douglas, had been an error of timing. Douglas was an American name, the name of a famous American general, because he was born at a time when the United

States was still a country to be admired. But soon after Douglas's birth, the United States abandoned Vietnam to the communists and Nixon was overthrown. And then James Carter, that useful idiot — useful to the communists — came to power. Carter, in the name of "human rights," had cut off aid to Guatemala, had allowed the Sandinistas to take over Nicaragua, and had overseen the overthrow of General Romero and the installation of the so-called revolutionary junta in El Salvador.

The three American nuns and their coreligionists were raped and killed on their way into San Salvador from the airport. Though President Reagan, a wise and good man, dropped the investigation into the deaths of the nuns, the U.S. Department of State nevertheless wanted names. It and the U.S. Embassy wanted the names of the men involved in the massacre, from high officers down to the enlisted men. They wanted names, just in case they needed scapegoats for their policies. Communist forces internal to the United States were trying to foment a scandal to bring Reagan down, and the State Department might one day have to prosecute those Salvadoran officers and soldiers in order to appease them. This was the contemptible weakness of the U.S. government, this eternal vulnerability to pressures from the communists. Eliott Abrams, the State Department's man in Latin America, had privately assured the Salvadoran Estado Mayor that it would never come to this. But then, Abrams was a treacherous Jew, of the kind who spit on Jesus Christ. The captain had been compelled to tell the Americans where the bodies were and then provide them with the names of those involved.

"They're trying to bring Reagan down the way they did Nixon," he said to his wife. "They even call the scandal 'gate,' like with Nixon."

Cecilia looked out at Texas and didn't answer. Politics didn't interest her.

The names, that's all the Americans wanted, the names. The captain was in a position to know all the names. That's what happened when you were a junior officer, you knew exactly whose lips gave the orders and whose fingers pulled the triggers. The captain was forced to deliver the names. In so doing he naturally betrayed certain colleagues, and inevitably the betrayed swore revenge on their betrayer. The Americans in turn offered the captain and his family protection under a witness protection program, but they would have to move to the United States and assume new identities. The Americans would send him to Texas, a big place to get lost in, and help him get started in the coffee import business, which he already knew something about. They politely declined his offer to become an officer in the American armed forces.

There had been a kind of consolation, as it were, in the choosing of new names for his family. For their new surname he chose Ponce, after his commanding officer, General José Emilio Ponce, himself a frequent target of the human rights campaigners. His son, Douglas, received the noble alias Maximiliano, after General Maximiliano Martínez, El Salvador's ablest historical figure, who in only two weeks in 1932 had cleansed the nation of thirty thousand subversives and gone on to rid the cities of disease by stringing colored lights across the streets. The captain became Napoleón. His wife could not be convinced to go with Margaret, after Margaret Thatcher, and instead chose, frivolously, Cecilia, just because she liked it.

They both liked the house in Northgate. Cecilia marveled at how everything worked, every fixture, every appliance, at the brush of a finger. She loved the big American bathrooms, but their unisex quality annoyed the captain, who had a bidet installed for her and a urinal for the men. Americans often don't know the difference between men and women, he said. Or between pets and children: look at those fluffy Lassie dogs that were always escaping from the neighbors' and parading down the streets, spoiled as princesses. He also had a forced-air hand drier put next to the sink, because it was more hygienic. Hygiene, as General Martínez had well known, was important. The captain especially liked the fact that all cables, electrical and otherwise, were buried at Northgate. He remembered the ugly day when the guerrillas pulled down the cables outside their El Salvador home: the downed wires had touched their razored fence and electrocuted one of the gardeners. Like a sissy, Max had wept over the man.

Max learned one day that his father imported more than coffee. He was waiting on the captain and the captain's three friends on the veranda, bringing them ice in a silver bucket and trays of Coca-Cola and lime wedges and bottles of Flor de Caña rum. "The Yankee government is stupid," the captain said, "with its ridiculous war on drugs. Coca, what is coca? Just a stimulant, like coffee. Things could as easily be the other way around, coffee illegal, coca legal. The coffee bean was in fact illegal in the Middle East for centuries!" The captain said he could as easily see himself smuggling illegal purified caffeine hidden in truckloads of legal coca leaves, as cocaine in truckloads of coffee beans.

The older, jowly man they called Pato cut his eyes to Max, lugubrious eyes white and red like raw pigs' knuckles. The captain, noticing the glance, said, "He's my son. No hay nadie de más confianza. Besides, I enjoy blanket protection from the Yankee government. I am untouchable."

The men nodded solemnly.

They sent Max to fetch the captain's camouflage-painted binoculars so they could spy on the bodies sunning by the lake. "Ah, qué gringos," said the captain. "The sun fascinates them. There they lie, roasting, trying to turn black as Indians." "¡Mira-mira-mira-mira-mira!" exclaimed the fat man they called the Panamanian. "One is naked as a grub." They wrested the binoculars from each other and took a look and then passed them to Max. "Look, Max, your first naked gringa! Go down there and grab her, Max! Get the gringuita, Max! ¡Atácala!"

Epimenio took the farm-to-market roads to Northgate. Last time he'd been in that area it had been to man a roadblock on the hardtop leading to Lake Hondo. The ostensible reason for the roadblock was to check vehicle registration, but everybody knew it was so the deputies could sniff for pot. The sheriff figured if you cut back on the pot smokers, you could cut back on the nekkidies. Epimenio had smelled a lot of pot that day, but he hadn't busted anybody, and he instructed the rookie with him to observe only, not search or arrest. They were just a bunch of college kids from Austin. You could read their lips — "shit!" — and see their brown arms pumping madly to open all the windows when they came over the hill and spotted the roadblock.

An ounce of prevention was better than a pound of cure. It was the same with speeders. Radar detectors enraged a lot of his fellow officers, especially the state troopers, but why? Wasn't the idea to slow folks down, and didn't the fuzzbusters do just that? All you had to do was turn your radar on and maintain a presence. Right now, as was always the case when he was in his squad car, he could feel the oncoming traffic recoil slightly when he came into view, while most of those behind him maintained a respectful distance. He sped up a little, so they wouldn't feel so cowed.

It was relaxing to drive the dips and twists of these Hill Country roads. It was almost exercise, the kind of exercise a sedentary man got. He thought of LBJ, home from the White House, tearing up and down these same roads in his old pickup, the Secret Service car squealing to keep up with him. Epimenio, a good driver who knew these hills as well as anybody, had once been assigned to drive ahead of the president, a kind of point man, without letting him catch up with him. That was truly the most exciting assignment he'd ever had, keeping ahead of the president of the United States bearing down on him at ninety miles an hour, a Secret Service agent beside him, smelling of nervous perspiration. Never let them tell you the Secret Service doesn't sweat, Epimenio always said after that.

This time he felt another sharp pang in his kidneys as he hit the dip at the bottom of a hill. He remembered Johnson's gall bladder operation, how he'd lifted his shirt before all the press to show the scar. He also picked his hound up by the ears. LBJ was a good ol' boy if there ever was one. And he had been anything but sedentary. He'd had the energy of a hundred men. Epimenio was proud of him, and to hell with Vietnam. And to hell with the accusations of corruption, which were nothing compared to Nixon and Watergate, or Reagan and Contragate. Domestically, LBJ had been one of the best things to ever happen to this country. He'd built these roads, and countless others. He'd electrified these hardscrabble counties. Lake Hondo, now a thin blue line on the horizon, was the result of one of those dams. Things were looking pretty good. The price of crude had hit twenty-seven dollars a barrel. The Northgate development already had a couple dozen homes built into the dozer-scarred limestone, though most of them were uninhabited and pure speculation.

Well, he'd been thinking about everything except how exactly to question the boy, and here he was already.

Deputy González drew up to a Bermuda grass lawn peopled with plaster saints and virgins and gnomes. This had to be the Ponce place. He was met at the door by a dark-skinned boy with hair cut military short and a startled, red-eyed look. And this had to be Max.

"The dogs," said the boy.

"Do you know whose dogs they are?" The deputy looked past the boy into the house, and eased his way in.

"I wanted to shoot them," said the boy.

The deputy spotted the pistol on the table.

The boy began to sob, his brown face rubbery.

"Why did you want to shoot them?"

The boy babbled and blubbered, something about a pit, dogs, dead nuns, soldiers, a war. My name isn't Max, I hate that name, our name isn't Ponce, we had to change our names and come here and I hate this place. The deputy didn't understand all of what he was saying; the accent wasn't Mexican, though, he knew that. Everybody at the sheriff's department expected him to understand Spanish perfectly, in every kind of accent, and to know everything everyone from south of the border was talking about, just because his name was Epimenio González.

Epimenio realized he had to piss bad: the tea and the tension were working together.

"Where's your toilet, m'hijo?"

The boy pointed down the hall. Epimenio reached it in a hobble: the pain in his kidney was like a hot spike. At least he had the presence of mind to palm the 9 mm; must be the father's. The bathroom was equipped with a urinal. Who in the world would install a urinal in his home bathroom? Epimenio laid the pistol on top of the forced-air hand drier. Who'd have *that* in his bathroom? He tried to urinate, but nothing happened except greater pain. He opened the medicine cabinet and looked for painkillers, but there was nothing like that there. He opened another cabinet, and the scent of coffee hit him. Behind the towels he found a large package tight with white powder and wrapped in tape. He squeezed it. Hurt radiated throughout his lower body. Dios mío, he was going to pass a stone right there. The pain focused his mind and made him understand the boy's words and see clearly what he had stumbled on: a wholesale amount of dope lying brazenly in the bathroom cabinet of a family in some kind of witness protection program.

The pain caused a brightness in his eyes like the popping of flashbulbs. He thought of the little guys who by chance triggered vast scandals, like the security guard who had caught the

Watergate burglars or the monkeylike Nicaraguan private who had shot down Hasenfus and opened up Contragate. He pictured himself at a congressional hearing, sweating under television lights. He heard himself repeating under oath how Sheriff MacPherson had given standing orders to his deputies to leave the Ponce family alone, but how he, Deputy González, had gone to the house one day after the boy had made a distressed and incoherent call to the station, and how the boy had blurted that they had come from some war-torn place and were living under assumed names. The deputy told the congressional committee how he'd then come across the cocaine in the bathroom as he searched for a painkiller for his kidney stone. He said the pain made him see it all immediately and clearly: Captain Ponce smuggling drugs with the complicity of the federal authorities assigned to protect him. He told the committee members that his being there before them was very much a déjà vu situation, because he had also foreseen, in that lucid moment, all that led up to these hearings: Sheriff MacPherson's quiet handing over of the cocaine to the feds, who then declined to prosecute; the deputy's telling Donna, the dispatcher, about it, and their agreeing that it wasn't right that kids were getting busted for a joint of pot down at the lake while this smuggler was trafficking hard stuff right under their noses, and Max not going to school but holed up miserably in that dope-laden house, playing with his father's guns, and nobody able to do anything about it; and the deputy told the committee how finally, under Donna's prodding, he had gone to the newspapers, and then the whole thing busted open, a sordid and tangled tale of murdered nuns and protected witnesses and drugs.

He heard a car pull into the driveway. He looked out the window and saw an elegant couple get out of a black Lincoln, glance with alarm at the patrol car, and start toward the house. The deputy managed to shut the cabinet door, then sank to his knees in agony. No, he didn't have to tell the sheriff anything, he didn't have to tell Donna anything. He was getting old, he had physical problems. He was no LBJ, he didn't have the strength or the personality to confront the sheriff and the Freddies and all the people who would try to stop him and ridicule him and accuse him of stirring up trouble in good times. The stone inched its excruciating way down his urethra. When would it be over, Lord? And then what? Would he take on the government, or would he cruise up the street, just a sedentary sheriff's deputy in a small Texas county, looking for two lost dogs?

Every Head's a World

My father and I are an hour out of El Paso, driving an old Ford pickup with a beat-up white camper shell, headed north to Albuquerque and I-40. To the west, the spires of the Organ Mountains rip holes in the clouds, and the road silvers with rain. My father chews Days O' Work tobacco, worrying it into his cheek, as I, just as deliberately, ease a little strip of newspaper out of my back jeans pocket.

The newspaper is in Spanish, my mother's tongue. I tore it earlier this morning from one of the bricks of marijuana my father and I and the sharp-faced man, Gómez, packed into the false bottom of the pickup, back in El Paso. I hold it in the dimness next to my thigh and try to make out the words. I can make out only the dateline: BOGOTÁ. Boogertown? A little snicker bursts from me.

"Why, for crying out loud," my father says, reaching over and snatching the piece of newspaper. His hand, wadding it up, poises in the air as if to smack me. Instead, he pops it in his mouth and chews it up. Then he cracks his door and lets the black oyster of newspaper and tobacco juice stream out on the speeding asphalt.

I know I have broken one of Gómez's rules: "What goes under, stays under." This means no trace of our secret cargo is ever to surface before delivery. We have border patrol checkpoints to pass through, and those agents' eyes are keen.

I slouch at my end of the seat and gaze sullenly into the side mirror, watching the streak disappear into the road, black on black. I'm glad. I'm glad I've done something risky. I'm kind of glad I've made him mad.

The sign announcing the checkpoint appears, set against the plush sand like the label at the bottom of one of my mother's pink velvet–lined jewelry boxes. My father shoves his chew deep into his cheek with his tongue and draws a deep breath. I jam my hand into my pocket and rub my tiny rabbit's foot.

The agent holds out his palm and we stop. He asks us our citizenship. "American," we say. He peers at me hard: I am much darker than my father, having inherited my mother's milk-chocolate skin. My father, on the other hand, is puro gringo, with eyes my mother called ojos de vidrio, because they are exactly the color of the famously flawed, handblown blue glass made in her hometown in Jalisco state. The agent looks again at my father, and my father's translucent eyes stare back at him, and the agent, unable to hold that gaze, waves us on.

"Yes!" my father hisses, once we are down the road, raising his fist and pulling it down.

His excitement frightens me. But I share his relief and let fly a playful punch to his shoulder. My bony thirteen-year-old fist sinks into his flesh. His arm has gotten flabby; he used to be able to haul two bales of hay in each hand.

As we drive into the soft gauze of rain, I begin to wonder

what would happen if the agents get a change of mind and come after us. What if my father doesn't stop? Will they shoot at us, shoot out the tires? I can picture the pickup plunging into that pink sand, sticking there nose down like some weird metal tombstone, the shell splitting wide open, scattering its contents all over the highway: a couple of old wooden chairs with puppy-gnawed feet, bundles of bright dollar-store clothes, and those sixty-six bricks of marijuana, strewn all over the road like the retread out there now.

"That retread gives me the willies," I say. It looks like roadkill, blood-black.

"Why's that?"

"I guess because I've never actually seen one fly off a wheel."

"Happens all the time."

"Yeah. But I just never seen it happen."

"Ever see an animal die?" I say. "You know, a wild animal?"

"Die all the time."

"Yeah. But you ever seen it happen?"

"I once saw a crow fall out of the sky, dead," he says, but a bounce of the truck knocks out the *r*.

"A *cow?*"

"*Crow*, smarty," he says, popping me on the crown of the head.

"Not shot or anything?"

"Not shot. Just dead."

"Must've had a heart attack."

He cracks his door and lets tobacco juice stream. I babble on: "I guess a guy can't keep from thinking."

"'Bout what?"

"'Bout . . . 'bout . . . you know . . . things."

He leers at me in a way that alarms me and makes a revolving motion with his hand. "The wheels just keep on turnin', don't they?" he says.

I lean my head back on the seat and hush.

*

My mother was happy the day before she died. More than happy: manic. Or to be more clinically correct, she was in the upswing of a bipolar event. She came into my room that Sunday morning singing her version of "El Tahur," that old song about the muchacho alegre, the gambling lad who wakes up singing too.

When she was elated, as she was then, she brought joy to our lives like nothing else could. She was in fact supposed to take her medication at times like these, but she didn't, and my father didn't make her. Why, he thought — we all thought — should she ruin her good moods? Why shouldn't she take the medicine only in her dark ones? We refused to believe this joy could be a part of her illness.

That morning her mood made me the muchacho alegre, the happy lad, and I felt like singing along with her. I kicked off my blanket and sauntered after her into the kitchen. My father sat spraddle-legged in the kitchen in his pajamas, laughing at something she'd said.

He turned to me. "Hey, pardner. Let's throw on our Sunday best and take your little jefa to Juárez."

Juárez lay only forty miles south of our Mesilla Valley farm. We had gone there on many other occasions of my mother's ecstasy, sometimes staying overnight at a motel, always eating sumptuously on the little money we had. If we had any money left over, my mother went shopping at the market, where the charm of her happiness won her some fine bargains, and at night she and my father would go dancing in the motel lounge. Sometimes my mother begged to go to more exotic places, especially Las Vegas — she felt lucky, she said, and ready for adventure. But she was always easy to dissuade from those extravagances, and so to Juárez it usually was.

Our favorite restaurant was a place of medieval-size furniture and animal heads on the walls, braziers piled with onions and chiles, and baby goat and suckling pig on spits. That after-

noon, as soon as my father lay snoring by the motel pool like a
sated knight, his farmer's tan bronze sleeves on his otherwise
pale body, my mother and I went off to the market. Shopping in
the United States bored me, but I loved to listen to her banter
and bargain with the marchantes in Mexico. That day, she came
away with three glittering scarves woven of metallic threads,
and a flashy red sequined gown. She had a lot more of this kind
of clothing at home, most of it stuffed into two large trunks in
the attic, and though my father sometimes got mad at her for
getting still more, usually he indulged her fancy, her fantasies.

That night, she put on the sequined gown and, laughing and
tugging my father's hand, took him dancing at the garish motel
nightclub. She looked more slender and diminutive than ever
in that tight dress. It was late when they got back. I was awakened by people whistling and jeering outside, and then my father unlocked the door roughly and pushed my mother in.

"That kind of behavior is just plain stupid," he said.

"Oh, leave me." She locked herself in the bathroom. In a few
minutes, I could smell marijuana smoke.

"Hey!" he yelled, banging on the bathroom door. "What the
hell do you think you're doing?"

No answer.

"You better get rid of that goddamned pot! Flush that shit
before I bust the door down!"

She opened the door and he grabbed what she had, and then
I heard the slow gurgle of the Mexican toilet.

"Pinche gringo," she said, suddenly vicious. "You don't know
how to have a good time. You don't know anything about life.
Life is an adventure! ¡La vida vale ser vivida! You don't even bet
on the roosters. You hiding on that little farm, you stick your
head in the dirt like that big estupid bird, what is the name, the
one they make the boots you say you too poor to buy —"

He slapped her then, and she gasped and was quiet. Those
were the last words I ever heard her speak. My father told me to

pack my bag, we were going home. I packed in the semidarkness, glancing frequently at my mother. She sat on the edge of the bed, staring at the rug, slowly wrapping each of the metallic scarves around her neck. Her movements were strange, and she looked strange in that red sequined dress with those scarves bulging around her neck. I knew she had begun to descend into her blackness, and I wanted to rush over there and throw my arms around her, but I didn't, partly because I didn't want to be interfering in their fight, but mostly because I knew her response to me would be distant, now that she had entered that downward spiral. I had tried affection at these times before, only to suffer her indifference.

The baler's rhythmic *ka-chunk-chunk, ka-chunk-chunk* woke me the next morning. We'd left the motel in the middle of the night, but my father had gotten up early to work the kinks out of that touchy machine. As soon as the sun burned the dew off, he would begin to bale the season's first cut of alfalfa. The Organ Mountains stood black and featureless against the gunmetal sheen of dawn. It was going to be another hot, limpid day.

I glimpsed my mother through the crack in their bedroom door. She lay on the bed in a fetal curl, breathing very lightly, still in her red dress, still with the scarves around her neck. I wondered if my father had even tried to undress her, or if he'd just let her be. I choked down my cereal, then went out to the highway to wait for the school bus. I watched my father way out there, his torso twisted around, glancing back at the beast as it swept hay up in its teeth and spat out a test bale. I waved, but he didn't see me.

For years afterward, I fantasized that my mother had gotten up that morning as happy as she had been the morning before, that she had flown out into the field to see my father and thrown her arms around his neck, and that that's how the accident happened, her scarves caught in the machine at the moment of their embrace. After that fantasy spent itself, I imagined her, more realistically, having changed into her work clothes to help him, and then getting pulled into the running baler when she foolishly or forgetfully reached into its maw. My father was himself careless in this regard. More than once I found one of his gloves packed tight in a bale.

Only much later would I learn what the life insurance company successfully argued in court after reviewing my mother's mental history: that her death was "at least eighty percent self-inflicted" and was preventable, had my father done the right thing and made sure she stayed on her medication.

By the time the school counselor pulled me out of class that morning and drove me home, the emergency people were gone and just a couple of sheriff's deputies remained, inspecting the baler. After the deputies left, my father backed the machine into the barn. He let the alfalfa go then, let it grow and grow until it flowered and lodged in a rough, dark sea of purple and green.

My father would not talk to me about my mother or her death. The space of her absence jelled around me like the pectin that thickened around the cactus fruit she used to make into preserves. My movements and my voice and my thoughts became sluggish and unreal. But my father went the opposite way. He became jerky and quick, as if he had drunk too much coffee. He went on a spending spree, borrowing money from the bank and getting everything from a new tractor to a new refrigerator with ice dispenser. He got us a VCR and a stack of action videos, an Amana microwave, and a Magic Chef stove with the ceramic-glass surface — that appliance wasn't just a stove, he said, it was a *range*. Not that we used that range much, since we ate men things, bachelor or widower things — Vienna sausages and tinned smoked oysters and tiny round cheeses in red rinds. I didn't have an appetite for these or anything else, but my father gorged on them compulsively and began to go to fat.

Despite the new machinery, he did hardly any work, and wouldn't tell me what to do, either. The alfalfa went to seed, the weeds grew tall in the pecan orchard, and the new field, which he had prepared to plant in pima cotton, remained fallow, turning the farm into a dust bowl every time the wind kicked up.

A loan got called in. My father took me to the bank with him.

The loan officer was a little man with a smooth, deep voice who sat behind a large oak desk. My father always said you could never trust a little man with a deep voice. He was so small and the desk so large he looked like a bust sitting on the edge of it.

The loan man rattled off many interesting phrases such as "negative cash flow," "land-hungry equipment," "no forbearance." He reminded us of the equipment we still owed on: one IH 1460 combine with cornhead, one 1978 Deere 770 with hydro, boom shaker for the pecans . . .

"Nestor," he said, "I'm sorry about everything, gosh darn I really am. But I have to level with you, we just can't let these loans roll over and play dead any longer."

My father cocked his head. "You can take the baler," he said. "Sir?"

"I said, you can take the baler. We're not cutting, so you can have the baler."

My father's big hands rested calmly on the armrests of his red leather chair, but the way his head was cocked and the peculiar twinkle in his eye made me sick.

The loan officer turned pale and looked down at his stubby fingers, which had stopped, in midair, their drumming on my father's promissory note. He mumbled something about keeping in touch, my father said "mighty fine," and they shook hands and I shook hands with the little man and we left.

"Shucks," my father said happily, sucking on a piece of beef jerky, as we sped along the flat roads. "That loan was in default before it was even written!"

*

My father met Mr. Gómez at a cockfight palenque near Columbus. The palenque was something my mother had always, when she was feeling adventurous and lucky, spoken of as the ultimate in betting. But it wasn't a place for women, and he had never gone himself, until now.

Gómez had a winning rooster. He also knew my mother's family, and knew who my father was. He introduced himself to my father. My father came home flush with beginner's-luck winnings and a nervous eagerness to begin some sort of business with Gómez. A few days later, Gómez drove to the farm in an old brick-red fifties pickup.

My social studies teacher, who was very interested in the subject of law enforcement, had just taught us a new word, "phrenology," which was the study of criminals by the shape of their heads, and I could tell straightaway that this Gómez would have been a phrenologist's delight. His forehead sloped back severely from his face, such that his eyes seemed too far up, like a flounder's. Everything about him was sharp: sharp nose, sharp chin, sharp look in his eye, hair sharply black and sharply cut and gleaming with something sticky. He even wore a sharply creased sharkskin suit, and finely pointed ostrich boots. Everything about the old pickup was rounded — opposite of him.

My father introduced me as his son and "partner." Gómez produced a feed sack with some seed at the bottom. The seed was shiny as mustard, smaller than okra. It would grow the best cash crop there ever was, he said.

"We give you ten dollars cash U.S. the pound." Gómez handed my father a business card. "You call here, you speak of cotton. You say, Yes, I grow cotton, I got cotton."

"I gotcha. Cotton."

"Yes. And we want only the females. You must kill the males early, when you see the little flowers. We want all girlie plants, and we want them virgins." He winked a narrow eye at me.

My face got hot. I had reached the age at which such talk

mortifies. I, who had witnessed the frightfully passionate mating of horses, had castrated calves, had made preg checks with my gloved arm deep in the vaginas of cows, was now embarrassed in the presence of mere talk. Gómez and my father let loose manly guffaws.

After Gómez left, my father made calculations in his head, based on the size Gómez said the plants were supposed to grow. We would make a fortune, he concluded. This wasn't just going to save us from foreclosure; we were going to have enough green left over, green dollars, to choke a cow. I must have looked a little scared because he stared at me straight on and said in a high voice, "Why, you're not afraid of a little adventure, are you, son? La vida vale ser vivida. Am I right or am I right?"

I felt a chill as I heard him speak, in that voice and that atrocious Spanish accent, those last words of my mother's.

"No," I whispered.

"Heck, no. I'll tell you what we're going to do. We're going to establish a little old trust fund for you so you can go to the college of your choice and study Spanish or wshatever the devil you want to. Now how does that grab you?"

We planted the seeds hidden among the pecan trees, and for the rest of the summer my father kicked back, drinking beer and eating the little cheeses and singing that song about Lucille, who picked a fine time to leave her husband, with a crop in the field and all.

He would sing it in a voice of dangerous sarcasm, carefully enunciating every syllable in a light tongue. And then he would laugh and mutter, "Big, dumb, sorry-ass redneck."

I put our old sorrel mare on double-feeds. She had gotten sick over the long, hot summer. She was twenty-four and had foaled seventeen times. My father, weary of her constant breeding, had put her last few foals out with the calves and the calves had licked and sucked the foals' tails until they were just slick green little nubs. When my father saw what I was doing, he took the feed pail gingerly out of my hand and sailed it away over the fence. A few days later, the mare died, the way horses do, stiff and scared-looking, and that same day my father loaded up the calves and the latest foal and took them to auction.

But sometimes my father was tender, as on the hottest of those hot nights, when he misted my sheets with cool spray from an atomizing bottle and said, "I hope you can sleep directly, but if you can't, just think of the cotton, how it's growing. That funny cotton likes it hot. It's just going to town."

But my father was wrong: the marijuana plants did not thrive. They became etiolated, starved for light, under the dense shade of the pecans. We harvested what few we had on a blazing Indian summer afternoon. We tossed them on the barn floor to dry, as Gómez had instructed us. It was shocking to behold how shriveled they became in a couple of days, the many-fingered leaves mummified into small, dark fists, the same way it had always shocked me to watch a pile of my mother's bright quelites cooking to an inky mass in the saucepan. When the marijuana plants were mostly dry, the tips of the branches still a little sticky, my father said it was time to run them through the baler.

I stood there, petrified.

"Go on, son, shove 'em in," he said in a tense voice, and climbed into the tractor cab.

I obeyed, pitching the plants quickly into that toothed maw. My father watched grimly, his face tight as dried leather, as three puny bales toppled out, giving off a resinous odor.

"All right, then, let's clean her out," he said wearily. "The repo men get to it like that, they'll know what's been through it. Buncha hopheads."

While my father went around to get the hose, I reached with dread into the baler's spiky mouth and pulled out the hemp fibers, which were wrapped tough as dental floss around those steel teeth. We hosed out the baler and then we went inside, where my father called Gómez while I mixed us a drink of Tang.

My father licked his orange-tinged lips and said to me, "We'll deliver tonight, pardner."

We tucked the three bales of marijuana in the forward part of the shelled pickup bed, and my father scattered mothballs to mask the sappy smell. More than mask it, they mingled with it, and it began to smell very much like my mother's clothes in the attic, that combination of sachet and naphtha. The same thought must have occurred to my father, because he came out of the house lugging the two trunks of my mother's clothes.

"Now if any uniformed man stops us and gives us a sniff," he explained, heaving the trunks into the bed, "these'll account for the mothball smell. You understand my thinking?"

"Yes, sir," I said in a small voice.

Gómez met us in a grove of cottonwoods on the banks of the Río Grande, in his sharkskin suit, smiling his lizardy smile. The smile disappeared when we showed him those three pale bales. He broke one of them open, sniffed, pulled his sharp nose away in disgust. He reached in, pulled something out. In his hand he held a little mass of pink skin and blood and tiny bones.

"What's that?" my father said dully.

Gómez went to the river and carefully rinsed his hands.

Weak-legged, I joined my father in examining the thing Gómez had pulled out. It was a crushed little baby rabbit. The baler must have pulled in a litter of rabbits nesting in the marijuana, or maybe they had been nesting in the baler itself.

Gómez came back and told my father flatly he didn't want the stuff. My father looked like he might reach out and snap him in half like a stick.

"Tranquil, tranquil," said Gómez, palms out. Our marijuana was no good, he insisted, but our "profile" was "tremendous." A farmer and his son in an old pickup: this was not what the police looked for when they looked for drug runners. So here was the new deal: we'd get rid of these bales, and then we would start running really good stuff, marijuana smuggled from Mexico, out of El Paso for Gómez. He handed my father a wad of good-faith money, which my father stuffed in his pants without counting.

We sat in silence on the bank of the Río for a long time after Gómez left, watching the soft animal body of the river slither past us. Finally, as night came, my father announced: "I ain't even gonna burn 'em. Let's just dump 'em."

I crawled in under the camper shell. I pushed the trunks aside and tipped the bales toward him. While my father took the first two to the river, I dug into the third and pulled out one of the baby rabbits. I cut off one of its tiny hind feet for luck with my pocket knife and tossed the crushed body out into the darkness.

He came back from the water out of breath and wild-faced. A person happening upon us then might have thought he'd just dumped a body. He snatched the third bale and in his other hand he grabbed one of the leather-handled trunks.

"You don't think I'm thinking straight, do you, son?"

"No. Yes. No, you are."

"You bet. We don't need both these trunks. All right? We need room for the new merchandise. We don't need two trunks. All right?"

"Okay," I whispered.

Down by the river, my father opened the trunk and let my mother's sequined gowns and embroidered blouses fall into the muddy water, where they swirled and pirouetted in the moonlight.

My father says again: "Yep, the wheels just keep on turnin'," and repeats that circular motion with his hand, to which an oncoming trucker responds in kind.

I know he wants me to talk, tell him what's on my mind. But

I don't feel I can talk to him about my fears. My father is doing what he's going to do, and nothing I say or do matters. I remember a saying of my mother's, Cada cabeza es un mundo, Every head's a world, a world unto itself. Maybe she said it as a way of explaining her illness, but now I finally come to realize that my father has a whole separate world in his head, too, a world now revolving around this thing he calls our adventure. And the last thing he wants to hear about is my dread. We are, for as long as I can foresee, going to be living this risk-filled life, the kind of life my mother, that manic last night of her life, derided him for shrinking from. And all I can do is sit here beside him and watch the road and count the retread and rub the shriveled rabbit's foot in my pocket, and try to build, in my own mind, a world of my own.

Tongue

"Chihuahua es una ciudad bella, antigua, colonial," Charles Patterson told his students as the bus whooshed through the chaotic traffic and dusty slums of Ciudad Juárez. He was eager to assure them that Chihuahua, the city to which they were speeding, was not as grim and ugly as the border town they were seeing here. It was he who had planned this year's Albuquerque Preparatory senior Spanish field trip to Mexico, and he felt responsible for making it a success. He was so keen on the four-day trip — after all, what better way to get students excited about a language than to take them to a country where everything was conducted in that language — that even when Prep's other Spanish teacher fell ill and couldn't go, he was able to persuade the administration that the trip truly required only one adult supervisor. Chihuahua was a mere day's bus ride from Albuquerque, he knew the route well, knew the hotel, had everything arranged. And the eight seniors who had signed up for the trip were mature. Take Gina Chávez, the Chicana, for example: with her own native speaker's command of Spanish, she was practically a coteacher.

"Sí, Chihuahua es preciosa, preciosísima," he said.

"Preciosa, preciosísima," came Gina's low, mocking voice from the back of the bus.

Patterson didn't mind his students making fun of him; their teasing seldom got to the point of undermining his authority. Nevertheless, he felt the balance between their affection and their contempt to be a delicate one. He believed that if he were physically just a little more gawky than he was already, a little more chinless and stooped, their natural teenage cruelty might go for his jugular, sin miramientos. And the fact that he was single, rather than dully married to an equally homely woman, gave him a necessary aura of mystery, he believed. Even his age, twenty-nine, favored the balance: like an older brother, he was someone they could treat familiarly, yet respect.

Much to Patterson's distress, the Prep students did not always show respect for one another. For example, the boys, for whom a girl couldn't be too rich or too thin, called plump Gina Thrifty Gina behind her back. Apparently the nickname derived from something they had learned about in biology class: the recent discovery of the so-called thrifty gene, the fat-conserving gene said to be possessed by Native Americans and their descendants. She reacted to the epithet by insisting all the more strongly on the purity of her Spanish blood. Her reaction disappointed Patterson, because in truth she was mestiza, part Indian, part Spanish — and probably more Indian than Spanish. To him, she was a lustrous beauty: sloe-eyed, skin like burnished pottery, her outrageously thick black hair twisted into a braid as fat and shiny as the high-gloss chain that swooped between the stone pillars of the school's driveway. Her plumpness, down to the stubby toes that peeked from her white sandals, was, to Patterson, delectable.

Gina and Emma sat together on the bus. Emma was Gina's

best friend. Emma the Emaciated, the boys called her, a nickname that in no way diminished their slavering adulation of her waiflike figure. Emma showed contempt for their adoration, and this in turn earned her Gina's admiration and allegiance.

Now Emma gestured at something outside the window, and Gina's hand shot up to hide her voluptuous lips before they bloomed in laughter. A fat man was riding a cottony white burro, his legs splayed, like Sancho Panza. Some of the other kids laughed too, and Patterson was gratified to see that something at last had broken the stunned silence brought about by the sight of so much squalor.

Patterson read aloud the immense red letters painted on the collapsing cinder-block wall of a vast junkyard: YONKE. Behind the wall stretched a sea of junked cars and twisted metal. "So what do we call that kind of word?"

"Spanglish," Tim said with a fake yawn, stretching his lanky body until his shirt rode up to his chest. His ribs seemed to circle him entirely, like a worm's segments.

"That's it. From the English 'junk.' And why not? It's a darned good word for the stuff. Just listen to it. *Junk*. Clunk, plunk. What could be junkier sounding? Of course, the true Spanish for it is just as good. Anybody know what it is?"

Gina gave the others a chance, and then murmured, "Chatarra."

"Chatarra," said Patterson. "Listen to it. You can almost hear that scrap metal being twisted and torn, can't you?"

The students stared out at the interminable scrapyard in silence. Patterson imagined they were recalling lurid tales of Mexican bus wrecks. Gina, in particular, wore an expression of exaggerated horror, as if to ask, What kind of country has this teacher brought us to? This dismayed Patterson, because if there was anything he wanted to come of this trip, it was Gina's appreciation of the land of her ancestors, a reconciliation with her mestiza blood. Patterson, believing he had talked enough, and feeling a little queasy from the lurching of the bus, took his seat.

As they sped through the hypnotically bright desert, Patterson daydreamed about his first trip to Mexico eleven years before, when he was eighteen and everybody still called him Charlie. The first part of that trip had taken him along this very road, the Pan-American Highway to Chihuahua. The journey had been his high school graduation present to himself: his parents had refused to bankroll his wandering alone in such a "dangerous" country, had even tried to bribe him out of the idea with promises of a new car. But the wheels he wanted didn't belong to a car in which to tool around his dull hometown of Omaha; they belonged to a crazy Mexican bus with chickens on the luggage rack and cumbias on the eight-track, bouncing its way to a tropical beach, the kind of bus he'd read about in Steinbeck and Kerouac.

That first bus he'd taken out of Juárez, however, was disappointingly first-class and would have been downright sedate if not for the dozen buoyant Mexican teenage schoolgirls it carried on their way back to Chihuahua from a visit to El Paso. Their uniforms were adorable: plaid skirts, white knee socks, saucy navy blue berets, black leather jackets over white blouses. The one in the seat directly in front of him suddenly turned her angelic face to him: What estate of the U.S. was he from?

She nestled her plump chin on the headrest and held the tip of her very red tongue seductively between her teeth as she listened, faintly amused, to his earnest efforts, in what he could muster of his high school Spanish, to describe Nebraska. Her eyes were bright and brown and her skin a luminous copper, and he could see, in the reflection of her window, her plaid-clad rump bouncing on her white-socked calves.

"Do you have a novia?" she asked, her tongue enunciating the Spanish fricatives with delicious delicacy before tucking itself back between those perfect teeth patiently to await his bumbling answer.

"No," he began, and was trying to formulate the words to tell her, without sounding too much like an idiot, that he in fact yearned to have a girlfriend, when the bus hit a pothole. He actually saw her teeth plunge into the soft redness of her tongue in the instant before her hand shot up to her wounded mouth. He drew an empathetic breath between his own teeth and reached up as if to touch her. Her classmates squealed with laughter.

"Eso lo ganaste por preguntona, Maribel," the teacher admonished her with a smile. "Ahora, siéntate bien."

Maribel obeyed her teacher and sat facing forward, but next to Charlie instead of in her own seat. Ignoring her classmates' murmurs and giggles, she continued the interrogation, dabbing a Kleenex every now and then to her tongue. She asked him about his friends and family, and told him about hers. The soft spots of blood dotting the tissue gave him a strange feeling in his heart. They talked about school, and she took his hands in hers and enumerated on his fingers the years in each phase of the Mexican educational system, so different from the American. A vaguely guavalike scent rose from her skin. When the desert night descended on them, and the only light remaining was from the star-pricks of the tiny bulbs strung along the luggage racks, he leaned closer to her to inhale her exotic fragrance and longed to soothe that wounded tongue, which pronounced so exquisitely the sounds of this lovely language, with his own . . .

"Mr. Patterson, oh, Pro-fes-sor!" That would be Gina's sardonic singsong rousing him from his reverie. "I think we're getting there, Professor!"

Patterson bolted in his seat, tugged the edges of his guayabera firmly over his lap, and looked around. Chihuahua already?

"¿Cómo se llama nuestro hotel?" Emma asked.

"Hotel Colonial," someone answered.

The bus roared into the heart of the city, jumped a curb, and lurched to a stop under the Colonial's ornate wrought-iron sign, which dangled like an old cobweb from the Egyptian-size volcanic tezontle rock of the façade. The inside of the hotel was just as Charlie remembered it: walls the same faded peach, the stone fountain bone-dry, even the same pudgy, ageless, eunuchlike bellhop peering at them with worry on his meaty brow. A broad double staircase snaked up from the lobby, intersected oddly with itself, and proceeded to the second floor. In colonial days, the lobby had apparently been an open-air courtyard, but now it was glassed in at the top with fiberglass that suffused it with a pale blue light.

"Looks like a harem," one of the boys remarked.

"Okay, you guys," said Patterson. "Figure out your rooms, get settled in, and we'll go out to eat."

"Me and Emma'll take the newlywed suite," said Jason.

"Oh, yeah, dream on, Jason," said Gina.

"Girls upstairs, boys down," Patterson ordered.

Patterson hurried to his own room, plopped his suitcase on the bed, and slipped back into the hall. He peered down a dim rear staircase: yes, there it was, the solid iron door, painted the same lurid pink as eleven years ago. He felt a stirring in his testicles. He stepped down to it and eased the metal bar through the sleeves: yes, exactly the same chirrido, the same squeak. The sound had the same effect on him now as it had had then: a kind of sweet terror.

Charlie, his head light with Maribel's departing promise to meet him at a certain Chihuahua city park the next afternoon, allowed a taxi to take him from the bus station to whatever hotel the taxi driver recommended. That hotel was the Colonial, and though it was more expensive than he had budgeted for, and the driver demanded too much for taking him there, he didn't care. The only thing that counted was the following day's date. He crept between the coarse sheets and breathed the ancient, stone-cooled air and listened to the vaguely threatening sounds of the Mexican night — an echo-chamber voice from a radio in another room, a derisive burst of laughter from the street, a faraway whistling in some unfamiliar code — and thought about Maribel, her bright eyes and copper skin, and her delicate tongue so cruelly wounded in the course of her conversation with him.

The next afternoon, as soon as Charlie and Maribel found a place to sit underneath the park's statue of a portly Pancho Villa, he asked to see that wound. It was still inflamed, but healing. He again felt a powerful urge to touch it with his own tongue, a desire that made his fingers and toes tingle. But he'd never kissed a girl like that and did not know how to go about proposing it. He saw couples kissing in the deeper shade of the park, and was working up the courage to suggest they retreat into those shadows, when she rose.

"I have to go," she said. "But we'll see each other again."

"When?"

"Tomorrow, here. At five." She gave his hand a squeeze and left.

He sat in the park a while longer, waiting for the tingling to subside and watching the other couples. Why so many? Parks in the United States didn't teem with lovers like this. He decided these folks had no other place to go. Mexico was so poor and crowded! People had no privacy here. He felt sorry for them, for these dark girls in print dresses who probably shared some wretched room with half a dozen siblings or were live-in servants in some despotic household that forbade them visitors. Probably the reason their boyfriends all kept those wide-brimmed cowboy hats stuck to their heads was to shield their girlfriends' faces, as they kissed, from the curious eyes of others — of people like him, he thought, suddenly realizing how intrusively he was watching them.

He drifted into a cavernous movie theater, hoping to distract himself with the James Bond film playing there. But again, it was as though he had stumbled into the makeout room of some vast teenage party. It was a festival of slurps and sighs, with no one paying any attention to the movie. Like parks, movie thea-ters in Mexico were perhaps one of the few places one could get away to be with one's lover. He tried to concentrate on the movie, but soon he left. When he got back to his hotel room, he felt the enormous emptiness of it. An enormous, lonely luxury that only a gringo could afford.

He lay on the broad bed and studied his guidebook, because if he was going to stay in Chihuahua a while, he'd have to find something more affordable. The book mentioned pensiones, private homes converted into boardinghouses, but warned that not much privacy was to be had in such places. The book said privacy, as a cultural concept, was much more valued in the United States than in Latin America. There was no good word in Spanish for "privacy," in fact. Moreover, said the guidebook, Mexico was a socially conservative country and American travelers sometimes found that the owners of pensiones, while providing a family atmosphere, put too many restrictions on their guests' activities: couples, unless they could prove they were married, could not room together, and sharp eyes were kept on outside visitors. Some hotels, especially provincial ones, flatly forbade guests to take visitors of the opposite sex to their rooms. Privacy could not be obtained even for a price.

He got up and wandered down to the lobby. The bellhop nodded at him with his permanent look of worry, and it occurred to Charlie that this might well be one of those conservative hotels the guidebook spoke of. It would be intensely embarrassing if, while escorting Maribel up the curving staircase, that bellhop were to call out and shake his bulldog head at him.

Charlie explored the hotel's corridors and staircases, hoping to find some unsupervised exit to the street. At the bottom of a rear stairwell stood a wrought-iron door painted a scandalous pink. He drew the bar: its squeak was awful in the night, but he drew it all the way and creaked open the door. It opened into a rubble-strewn alley. Behind the alley was the street. Perfect. He could let her in through here. He creaked the door shut again and drew the bar. He looked around. No lights had come on, no one had heard that sweetly terrifying music. He trembled with anticipation.

At breakfast the next morning, Emma announced she'd had a terrible night. The double bed she'd shared with Gina — a boy would have never shared a bed with another boy, but the girls considered that kind of thing an act of sophistication — was unbearably lumpy.

"Well, how did you sleep, Gina?" Patterson asked.

"Oh, she slept like a baby," Emma interjected with a wave of her limp hand.

"Princess-and-the-pea and Rip Van Winkle share the sack," said Tim.

"Shut up, Tim," said Emma and Gina at the same time.

"We've got like this extra trundle bed thingee in our room," one of the other girls volunteered. "It's like really narrow, but it's firm."

"Narrow shouldn't be a problem for Emma," a boy said.

Emma turned to Gina. "You don't mind having our room all to yourself tonight, do you, dearie?"

"No," Gina said petulantly.

"She's her own padding," Tim whispered to Jason, and they giggled.

After breakfast, Patterson spotted two young Mexican men — boys, really — chatting with Emma and Gina in the lobby. From their little folded-newspaper hats and dusty clothes he deduced they were a couple of the albañiles working on the restoration of the hotel's south side, whose ringing chisels had awakened him that morning. Delighted to see his students conversing with the natives, as it were, he lingered by the water cooler to catch what they were saying. He hoped the boys would keep it decent: albañiles — stonemasons and bricklayers — were proverbially the most coarse-tongued of all workers, like truck drivers in the United States.

"¿Qué van a visitar hoy?" asked the dark, long-lashed boy. He had a high-bridged nose and amused eyes and a broad smile, and looked very Indian. The other boy was stockier, with a ruddy complexion not unusual in Chihuahua, a sign of the Mennonites and Anglo cowboys and miners who had wandered into the region over the centuries.

"Museo Pancho Villa," said Emma.

"¡Ah! ¡El Museo de la Revolución!" said the dark boy. "¡Muy interesante!"

Emma, though her Spanish was nowhere near Gina's, carried the girls' end of the conversation. No, they didn't have boyfriends; did he and his friend have girlfriends? No? Emma laughed her flirtatious laugh. Yes, their teacher was simpático, muy simpático. They'd be here two more days, dos.

"Okay, Em, I guess we'd better get ready to go," said Gina in English, tugging on her sleeve.

"¡Ay, qué buena está!" growled the dark boy as they watched the girls head to their room.

Qué buena está: how good she is. But not good in the sense of virtuous, because that would be "qué buena es." What the boy meant was, what a looker she is. Now there was a good lesson in the two forms of the Spanish verb "to be," one that would get his students' attention. But which girl was the boy referring to, Emma or Gina? Had to be Emma, the elfin, exotic gringa, the one who talked so coyly with them, the girl all boys liked.

The Museo Histórico de la Revolución turned out to be muy interesante mostly to Patterson's male students, whose "too cool!"s rang out every time they encountered another Hotchkiss machine gun or Gatling gun or one of Pancho Villa's old cars, especially the one he was assassinated in. The girls, meanwhile, debated over which of the Mexican revolutionaries was the best-looking. Gina reluctantly agreed that Zapata might well be considered a fox, but didn't think Villa was attractive at all.

"He's just gross and fat," she said.

"But look at him here with his wife," said Emma. "I think they're *cute*."

"Plump," said Patterson, coming up behind them. "Plump is sexy."

He heard a boy groan. Gina whirled around and stared at him. He felt himself blush and, walking on, fell back on his favorite phrase whenever he put his foot in his mouth in front of his students: "Okay, chicos, todo en español."

That evening, Patterson took the students to the pedestrian mall near the hotel where the young people of Chihuahua gathered every night to laugh and flirt. As soon as they got there, most of his kids headed straight into the sparkling Woolworth's for all-American sundaes and splits (the hotel restaurant offered only objectionable Mexican desserts like flan and jellied quince). Emma, predictably expressing a haughty disgust at the idea of more food, gathered her long bones onto a wrought-iron bench by the fountain, accompanied by the ever-loyal Gina. Patterson went to a nearby newsstand, from which he could simultaneously peruse the weeklies and keep an eye on his wards.

It was eight o'clock, the height of the cruising hour, and people streamed up and down the concourse. Mexican boys eddied around the two girls. Eventually, one of them made a courtly request to sit with them. Patterson recognized him as the dark-skinned young stonemason who had spoken to them after breakfast this morning. The boy now wore brand-new blue jeans and a pearl-buttoned Western shirt and cowboy boots with silver toes. A high-crowned white felt hat had replaced his three-cornered newspaper one.

Because Patterson was so used to Emma, rather than Gina, being the center of boys' attentions, he assumed Gina was acting merely as an interpreter between Emma and the boy. But when Patterson edged a little closer, he saw the boy's attention was focused on Gina. Emma was looking away from them, a bemused smile on her face.

Patterson exulted. The Mexican boy had chosen the plump Chicana mestiza over the anorectic Anglo.

His other students bounced out of Woolworth's full of sugar and energy. Jason produced his beloved Hacky Sack, and he and Tim began to play. Some Mexican boys soon joined in the game. The girls went window-shopping, and it wasn't long before they were surrounded by their own jocular Mexican admirers. Emma joined the other girls, leaving Gina alone on the bench with the boy, and after a while Gina stopped looking around for her, drawn in by whatever the boy was so earnestly telling her. And the other students paid no attention to Gina, though Patterson believed he heard a wry American boy's voice, woven like a deeper thread in the brighter hum of Spanish, say, "Hey, man, plump is sexy."

The day of Charlie's second date, if these meetings with Maribel in the park could be called dates, was one of the longest Charlie could remember. Too nervous to have an appetite, he skipped lunch and strolled aimlessly around town. He didn't know what to expect of this second rendezvous, but he did not think he could kiss her in the park, with people watching. What if one of those people happened to be a brother, or a jealous suitor? No, it would be better to suggest they go to his hotel.

An hour or so before his appointment with Maribel, he wandered through the swinging doors of a bar. A beer would help calm him.

"¡Amigo!" a hoarse voice called from a table. "I invite you!"

Over the years of his subsequent travels in Mexico, Patterson would learn the protocols of gracefully declining the binges to which Mexican men invariably invited him whenever he entered a bar: the appropriately humble "con todo respeto, otro día, mi amigo," or the ploy whereby he would invite others before they could invite him and thereby retain the power to quit the party without offending anyone. But he didn't know these things then, and he timidly thanked the scruffy men and sat with them. He was not used to drinking, and by the time his third beer materialized in front of him, he was desperate to find a way out without insulting his glassy-eyed hosts.

"¿La hora? ¿La hora?" he said, trying to impress upon them that he needed to be somewhere soon. In fact, he had a watch in his pocket, but he was afraid if he looked at it, one of them might take it from him. He glanced at the bartender, but the man continued to dry mugs noncommittally.

"Mexicans don't look at the time," one of the men said gruffly. "This is México!"

Charlie excused himself to go to the toilet and slipped out the back door of the cantina. Leaping over puddles that stank of urine and stale beer, he reached the street that led to the park. As it happened, it was Maribel who was late.

"Fuchi, you smell of swill," she said, tugging him awake. The combination of beer and afternoon heat had made him nod off on the steps of the statue.

He felt dazed. The mineral hills behind her lovely, disapproving face were a blur of ocher and rose.

"Maribel," he said, taking both her hands in his. "Maribel, it's too hot here. Don't you want to go to my room?"

She unraveled his fingers from hers, crossed her arms, and stared into the distance.

"I don't go to hotels."

"It's a nice hotel," he bumbled on. "You don't have to go through the lobby. There's a door in the back I can let you in. It's a nice room."

"I don't go to hotels! What do you think I am?"

He tried to explain that he didn't mean anything untoward by it, that he was seeking only what gringos called privacy, didn't she know what privacy was? The more he talked, the worse it sounded. Metiendo la pata, putting your foot in it, was what the Mexicans called it. She got up, and, with an indignant downward brush of her plaid skirt and the words "I am decent!" stalked off.

Stunned by his mistake and her venom, he didn't react immediately. Then he bolted from the steps and went after her, but it was too late: she had disappeared into the crowd pouring out of the James Bond movie.

Charlie wandered back to the Colonial in a state of shock. He crept into bed. His skin felt cold, reptilian. He struck himself hard on the side of the head with his fist, but this did not awaken in him a sense that he had said anything really wrong. It didn't seem so bad to ask a girl to one's place, wherever that place might be, not a girl who seemed to like him as much as Maribel. Even if he had been stone sober he might have ventured the suggestion. No girl back home would have taken such umbrage at it, but as the men at the bar said, this was Mexico.

He lay on his bed and, in the dying light of day coming through the bathroom's frosted window, looked up her last name, Sánchez, in the Chihuahua white pages. There were three pages of Sánchezes. But even if he were to start to call them all until he found Maribel, there was no guarantee that he could fix things. Maybe he'd only make them worse. Maybe in Mexico a boy didn't call a girl at home. He let the phone book fall to the floor. The same derisive laughter and strange whistling as he'd heard the night before rose from the street. He realized then he had no idea where he was. He didn't know the signs or the words, the customs or the culture, and tears of loneliness and frustration crept into his eyes.

*

Gina came down to breakfast bright-eyed, as if she hadn't stayed up half the night, as Patterson knew she had, talking with Emma. She was more made up than usual, with mascara she didn't need and purple lipstick. Emma joined her and, though obviously sleepy, gamely listened to Gina's chatter. Gina kept her eyes on the entrance to the patio and turned frequently to look out the window that faced the street. Then she apparently saw who she'd been watching for, and grabbed Emma's hand: "Oh, shit."

The dark-skinned boy, again in his dusty overalls and three-cornered newspaper hat, stood at the entrance to the restaurant. Patterson wondered why he hesitated to come in, and then realized it was because he, Patterson, the chaperon, was staring at him. Patterson turned back to his coffee, but out of the corner of his eye saw the boy wave in Gina and Emma's direction before disappearing back into the street. Patterson glanced at the girls and saw them both silently, simultaneously, mouth the words "*so cute.*" Gina squeezed her friend's bony fingers, drew a big breath into her ample chest, and looked up to the sky like a stricken saint.

Again that evening, Patterson acquiesced to popular demand and took the class back to Woolworth's and the pedestrian mall. As he might have foreseen, the dark boy was already there, waiting for Gina. Emma again left them alone on the bench and joined the others in Woolworth's, and, much to Patterson's surprise, gobbled an enormous double sundae.

The Prep boys, emerging from Woolworth's, nudged each other when they saw Gina on the bench with her friend, but soon got wrapped up in their Hacky Sack game and forgot about her. Emma, meanwhile, seemed almost to be distracting the other girls from becoming too curious about Gina and the boy. Patterson couldn't be sure from his post at the magazine stand, but it seemed to him those two were sneaking some hand-holding in the darkness.

When Gina and her friend finally got up to stroll the mall — it must have been eleven o'clock by then — Patterson shadowed them. Instead of turning where the stores ended and coming back, they continued in the direction of the Hotel Colonial and around to its south side. At first Patterson believed the boy was showing her the stone he chiseled, and perhaps he was. But then he made a pulling motion with his hands and seemed to wait for an answer. Finally she nodded, and he took her into the shadows and kissed her. Then, perhaps fearful of raising suspicions, they hurried back to the mall.

"Okay, chicos, a acostarse," Patterson said, ordering his students back to the hotel. He had broken into a sweat following Gina and the boy.

They booed, but trudged obediently back to the hotel and to their respective rooms. Of course, this was exactly what Gina and the boy wanted, if he had read the boy's gesture correctly: that everyone be tucked into their rooms so she could then sneak down and draw the bar to the pink door and let him in.

Patterson paced his room, unsure of what to do. What he should do, as a proper teacher, was march straight down the hall, let Gina know what he'd seen, and warn her of the consequences of any shenanigans. And then go down to the front desk and insist that they padlock the pink door.

But he didn't, and later he would have much time to reflect on why he hadn't, because not long after their return to Albuquerque Gina ran away from home and went back to Chihuahua and eloped with the stonemason, and Patterson's contract was not renewed for the following school year. On his best days, Patterson believed he had done nothing but respectfully allow Gina the freedom to make her own decisions. When he was depressed, he told himself he had, out of sheer prurience, seduced her vicariously through the stonemason. At yet other times he justified his inaction by saying far be it from him, an Anglo, to have attempted to interfere with love between this Mexican and this Chicana, these two members of la raza; and then he would tell himself that this smacked of resentment for his own failures in the art of seduction, not only with Maribel but also with every other Latina woman he had tried to connect with in that way, even after years of studying Spanish. In the end, all he knew was the facts of that night. That he slipped between the heavy sheets of his bed and listened. He listened for the distant squeak of the bar on the pink door being gingerly drawn. He listened, over the thumping of his heart, for proof that blood had called to blood, that the Mexican stonemason, the golden-tongued albañil, had found the right words to seduce the Chicana.

Trial Day

"When did you first notice your brakes making the grinding noise, Mr. García?" the attorney for Brake Time asked Donaldo.

Donaldo García, the plaintiff in this civil action and a lawyer himself, rose to his feet in the witness stand. "Objection. Irrelevant."

"See?" said the judge to the ceiling, amused. "This is what happens when we get lawyers pro se: *the witness objects." He waved García down and turned to the Brake Time attorney. "All we need to do, sir, is ascertain the repairs Mr. García asked your client to make to his car versus those your client did in fact do, so I'm going to sustain the objection."*

"Your Honor, I'm simply trying to establish Mr. García's frame of mind when he took his car in to my client. According to my client, the shoes had cut into the drums rather deeply, which means the noise must have existed for some time. Now, it's my feeling and belief that because Mr. García had just recently be-

gun his career as a lawyer, he was under a good deal of stress, and simply did not notice the noise, or chose not to notice it, until the morning when he pulled into my client's garage all in a fluster and ordered him to fix the problem and basically any other problems the car might have."

"Your feeling and belief?" García cried. "Judge, that's the purest speculation —"

"Sustained!"

Donaldo García, greenhorn lawyer, mano a mano against the Brake Time franchise and its powerful corporate counsel. And García was winning. Naturally, in a fantasy such as this, it was easy to be before a sympathetic judge. In point of fact, García, the newest public defender in Coronado County, New Mexico, didn't know any of the civil judges, who inhabited the rarefied top floor of the courthouse, as if money disputes were loftier than criminal complaints. Custody arraignments, on the other hand, were held in the stuffy and windowless basement, which was where García was at the moment, waiting for his cases to be called. If one didn't know he was deep in a day-dream, one would believe he was simply entranced by the swirling tattoos on the ox-broad neck of the hung-headed prisoner being arraigned in front of him.

"Yoo-hoo, Counselor, you're up-up-up," said Molly, a fellow PD, waving her palm in his face.

García jumped to his feet and approached the bench. "We'd like to waive a formal reading of the indictment, Your Honor."

The judge, as sardonic as the one in García's fantasy, regarded him with a smirk. "And so, probably, would we all, Mr. — what is it?"

"García, Your Honor."

"Mr. García, but you see, the State hasn't had a chance yet to inform your client what the charges are. Now, relax, Counsel. You're doing ju-ust fine."

García could sense behind him what he had come to call the "tableau vivant" — that phenomenon wherein all movement and conversation at the defense's and prosecutors' tables, and even among the prisoners and spectators, would freeze as everyone's attention was drawn to this judge's famous put-downs. The court reporter swung her head up to look at García's darkening face, her smoothly noncommittal gaze now flawed by a nick of derision.

The prosecutor proceeded to list the charges. García argued unsuccessfully for a lower bond. The tableau dissolved. The transport officers whisked the prisoner back to the jail, and García ducked back to the defense table, where his thoughts wandered once again to the Brake Time dilemma.

The imaginary Brake Time lawyer was correct when he said García had ignored the brake noise until this morning on his way to the courthouse. After first speeding up to beat a red light, he slammed on the brakes at the last instant. The brakes screeched hideously, metal tearing into metal. Annoyed by his hesitation at the light — indecisiveness was one of his character flaws, he knew that — and appalled at the sound, he pulled, decisively now, into the Brake Time shop a block from the courthouse.

"You could probably hear me coming," he told the lanky man with the name Ray embroidered above the pocket of his overalls.

Ray's pupils were a bit too large and his movements too quick for seven-thirty in the morning, and García recalled Molly telling him that methamphetamine use was way up for young working-class whites.

"Cuttin' into the drums?" Ray asked.

"Yeah," said García. "I mean, I guess." You didn't want mechanics to know you didn't know diddly about cars, but you didn't want to act too smart, either, lest they test you.

A door opened behind Ray, and a short and paunchy middle-aged man with rather pompous sideburns emerged from an office. A flywheel and various pistons lay on the office desk, like enormous paperweights.

"I'm Bill Johnson," he said, offering his hand. He looked García's nailhead suit up and down and said, "You an attorney?"

"Right," said García. "Public defender. Headed over to the courthouse right now. Arraignments."

"We get a lot of attorneys here."

"Well, it's convenient."

Bill took a form as multiple as an arrest warrant from behind the counter. "So what do you see the most of?" he asked as García filled out his name and address. "Case-wise."

"Oh . . . Possession of controlled substances. Driving while intoxicated. I've got a DWI trial this afternoon."

"Is that a fact?" Bill looked at García straight on. His eyes were small and gray. "I guess they're your bread and butter, them drunks."

García shrugged. "I really don't know. I haven't been practicing very long."

"Fresh out of law school, huh?"

García thought he detected scorn in Bill's voice and hoped it was just his own paranoia about what people thought of lawyers. He glanced up at the clock: its hands, the wrench-wielding arms of the Brake Man mascot, said it was nearly eight.

"Okay," said Bill, getting down to business. "You're gonna need good brakes to avoid all your drunks. So let me tell you what we've got."

Bill described some kind of special semimetallic friction lining, as well as the possibility of having to regrind the drums if the shoes had cut into them bad.

"Of course, we do everything here, not just brakes," Bill went on. "Don't let the sign fool you. We can run a diagnostic on her and then call you if we find anything else wrong."

"I'll be tied up in court all morning, is the thing. I mean, I won't be in my office."

"You got a beeper?"

"No, no beeper."

"Most of your lawyers will carry a beeper, if not a cell. Okay, well, you call us, then."

"Okay," García said as he headed out the door. "I'll try."

Mechanics made him nervous. He didn't know why, but they cowed him. So cocksure. People thought lawyers were bad that way, but mechanics were worse. He shouldn't have said he hadn't been practicing long. He should've told Bill he specialized in consumer law and deceptive trade practices. Semimetallic lining, was it? Well, maybe that was a good thing to have. What did he know? Obviously, he needed some kind of brake work done. It was good to be able to stop. But he should have been firmer. He should have said, "Don't do anything until we talk about it." Because what did "I'll try to call" mean to Bill? Was it tacit approval to repair whatever the diagnostic came up with?

"So, Mr. García," said the Brake Time lawyer, "if you were so worried about the work my client was to do on your car why didn't you call?"

"Well, I could hardly use the clerk's phone for private business. We were in arraignments."

"Wouldn't look good, would it, especially your being so fresh on the job? I think we can all understand that. But couldn't you have stepped out to the phone bank in the hall?"

"I didn't know when my cases were going to be called. The judge was skipping around on the docket. Besides, I didn't have a quarter."

García realized he'd just perjured himself by saying he didn't have a quarter, and his guts turned to ice.

"Didn't have a quarter? Didn't have a quarter in your pocket? Wasn't Molly, your colleague, fellow PD, right there? Couldn't you have turned to her and asked her to cover for you while you stepped out to make the call? Ask her for a quarter, if you didn't have one?"

The son of a bitch was very, very good. Yes, Molly was right there, and she probably would cover for him. And he *did* have a quarter in his pocket, in fact he was running his fingernail over its milling as he considered going out to the hall and calling Bill at Brake Time.

"Here's my theory," said the Brake Time lawyer in his closing arguments. "My theory is that Mr. García wanted something to distract him that morning. Something to keep his mind off the DWI trial he had coming up that afternoon. A bench trial, but nevertheless his first trial ever. Mr. García knows himself. He knew that if he dwelled on the trial he would get unduly nervous. It was a simple case, he had prepared for it as best he could, and he knew that he should not obsess on it, that he should keep his thoughts elsewhere until the time came. And the perfect foil for his distraction was Bill Johnson and Brake Time and the work they needed to do on his car. Meanwhile, Mr. Johnson's morning is tied up waiting for Mr. García's call. Mr. Johnson, in short, was the unsuspecting victim of a psychological game Mr. García was playing in his own mind for his own selfish reasons . . ."

That was enough. García palmed the quarter from his pocket and looked around for Molly, to get her to cover for him while he made the call. But she had already picked up her files and was heading out the door.

"You coming to Los Hermanos with us for lunch?" she said before he could open his mouth. "Great posole. Meet us in the lobby at twelve; don't be late."

Five PDS were gathered at noon in the courthouse lobby when García, out of breath, joined them. They agreed they didn't have much time, this being zoo day and all, but they still wanted to go to Los Hermanos, for the posole and the tamales. García still hadn't made his phone call, but he told himself he could do that from the restaurant.

"So how's it going, Donaldo?" one of them asked him, once they'd all settled in their booth. "Ready for trial?"

García said he was as ready as he was going to be. He was going to argue that the police hadn't read his client, a Mexican national by the name of Rodríguez, the Implied Consent Act before they did the Breathalyzer test on him. Or, at least, they hadn't read it to him in any way that Mr. Rodríguez understood, his knowledge of English being limited.

"How limited?" Molly asked.

"Well," said García, "he understands *me* okay."

"But you can talk to him in Spanish."

"Actually, no," said García, feeling heat in his face. "I don't speak Spanish. He speaks some English, though."

"But you're bringing in the Spanish interpreter, right?"

"Of course."

Everyone agreed that it was worth a try. García's embarrassment receded; the heat he felt now was the warmth of their approval.

"One caveat," said Molly. "Old Judge Wallace — you say it's a bench trial before Wallace, right? — she's not big on the don't-understand-English defense. So make sure you woodshed your Mr. Rodríguez to play real dumb. He knows only Spanish. Not a peep of English."

This, García thought, is what he liked about being a public defender. The PDs formed a pool of knowledge, of resources, unmatched anywhere except perhaps at the largest law firms. Maybe none of them would ever become hotshot private trial lawyers, but as a community of shared experience they were hard to beat. He took a bite of his tamale — the red chile was rich and smooth — and felt content.

"Speaking of implied consent," he said, "I dropped my car off at the shop without making it very clear what I wanted, or didn't want, done on it. I guess I'd better call to see what's up."

"What shop's that?"

"Oh, this Brake Time place down the street from the courthouse."

Molly asked the others, "Wasn't that the guy whose kid was killed by the drunk driver last Christmas?"

García settled back into his seat, gingerly. He could feel its sponginess.

"Johnson, yeah," someone said. "The defendant was named something like Simpson. Stinson. Driving a Jaguar, coming back from the opera in Santa Fe. Didn't have a scratch. Remember that? He hired like the whole Grayson and Carr boutique. They got the depraved-mind murder tossed, and the guy pled out to agg DWI. Got probation."

"Now the victim's mother, Mrs. Johnson, is a MADD activist," said Molly. She turned to García. "Don't be surprised if she and her people show up at your trial. They're the folks in the purple-and-white T-shirts. The judges are scared shitless of them, and they'll let them put their two cents in at sentencing."

García stirred his iced tea slowly. At times like this, the world seemed too dense with contingencies. Once again, he felt adrift and indecisive. He couldn't bring himself to get up and go to the telephone and make the call. In their hurried departure from the restaurant, he hesitated idiotically by the table, fingering the quarter in his pocket and wondering if he should throw it in with the tip. "Ready, Counselor?" Molly called. As he passed the cashier, he grabbed a fistful of mints and shoved them in his pocket.

His client, Mr. Rodríguez, was waiting for him on the courthouse steps. García was glad he'd picked up the mints, because Rodríguez's breath smelled of alcohol. Some of the prisoners being arraigned, García had noticed, carried toothbrushes in the pockets of their jail jumpsuits — pathetic, really, since dental hygiene was the least of their problems at the moment. But it showed some kind of foresight, and García had hope for them. This Mr. Rodríguez, on the other hand, had not even thought to desist from drinking on the day of his drunk-driving trial. Maybe he'd driven here, too. But at least he'd shown up. García gave him a mint and ushered him into the courthouse.

Mr. Rodríguez had the same first name as his lawyer — Donaldo. Client Donaldo learned this at their first interview and was extremely impressed. "We are tocayos!" he kept saying. Afterward, attorney Donaldo asked one of the court interpreters what that meant, tocayos, and the interpreter said it meant they had the same nombre de pila, or first name, which was kind of a magical thing in Mexican culture and meant a special bond existed between them.

García didn't feel any special bond with his client, however. Mr. Rodríguez was an unemployed laborer and alcoholic from a state in Mexico that García had never heard of; García was raised in a nearly all-White suburb of Denver. The Garcías had been in Colorado for generations, spoke only English, rarely even ate Mexican food. Donaldo García, named after his grandfather, in fact hated his first name. He would have liked to drop the final *o*, but then that would leave him with the name of a famous duck, and he was self-conscious enough already of the bill-like swoop of his long nose. "Don" would be all right, though; it had a kind of elegant ring. He really should have introduced himself as Don to everyone when he started working here. It would take about five minutes upstairs in civil court to have it legally changed to Don, but he would have to muster a certain decisiveness he knew he didn't have.

García followed Molly's advice and told Mr. Rodríguez to wait until the Spanish interpreter finished interpreting the questions before he answered, even if he understood the English. They entered the courtroom. García glanced at the people in the spectators' gallery, but there was no one there in a purple-and-white T-shirt, thank God.

Judge Wallace was notoriously down-home. She hailed from a remote part of New Mexico and spoke with a Texas twang. She was due to retire next year, and apparently didn't much care what people thought of her.

"So we got a trial right at siesta time," she said, leaning back in her massive leather chair. She picked her teeth with the corner of a business card. "Well, let's get on with it."

It started off excellently for García. The arresting officer admitted that he couldn't be sure the man sitting before them, Mr. Rodríguez, was the driver of the pickup.

García put on the face of incredulity he had often practiced in front of the mirror in anticipation of just such an opportunity.

"You stopped a vehicle on suspicion that the driver was intoxicated and you don't know who the driver was?"

"When they saw me, they sped up and I lost them around a bend. That's an unlit area, and it was extremely dark. By the time I caught up with them they were stuck in the sand by the roadside and were out of the vehicle, trying to push it."

"Who is 'they'?"

"Three HMAs. Hispanic male adults."

"How do you know my client, Mr. Rodríguez, was the driver?"

"He said so."

García called Rodríguez to the stand. He had his fingers crossed that the man would do as he'd coached him and wait for the Spanish interpreter to finish interpreting the questions. Rodríguez did great. García gazed out the courtroom window as his client, always waiting for the interpreter to finish the question, gave the answers García wanted to hear. No, he didn't understand the officer when the officer asked him to walk nine steps, touching heel to toe. No, he didn't understand the officer when the officer read the consent decree and asked him if he consented to take the breath test. García was vaguely aware that he was looking out at the barren badlands beyond the city's western edge. But mostly he was aware of an odd but delicious tingling in his chest: a sensation of imminent victory. At one point, he found himself actually rocking on his heels with delight.

Then Judge Wallace said abruptly to his client, "Let me ask you just one thing."

Mr. Rodríguez turned in the witness box to face her, and García could see his fright as he was suddenly confronted with her huge, doughy face.

"Were you driving the truck that night?"

Again Mr. Rodríguez waited patiently for the interpretation and then answered: "I don't remember."

"You don't remember if you were driving?"

"Objection, Your Honor!" cried García, appalled that the judge would interrupt his direct like this. "Asked and answered!"

"Overruled. You don't remember whether you were driving the truck that night, Mr. Rodríguez?"

"I don't remember! I was drunk!"

This brought down the house; and with it, García's hope for an easy acquittal.

"Did you understand the officer that night when he asked you if you were the driver?" the judge asked Rodríguez.

Before the interpreter had a chance to interpret the question, Rodríguez blurted, in English: "No! He speak to me in English! I no understand English!"

Again the courtroom erupted in laughter. The judge showed her tiny, stained teeth.

"Case closed," she said, leaning back with satisfaction. "This man understands English perfectly well. Otherwise he would have waited for the translation before answering."

"But, Your Honor, understanding what you just said is a far cry from understanding the language of the consent decree! Your Honor, may I read him that language so we can see if he has any idea . . ."

The judge, swiveling in her chair, savoring her trick, wasn't listening to him. She surveyed the courtroom and pointed to someone in the back. "Officer Tyler, you're grinning."

"All right, Mr. García, hang on to your hat," Judge Wallace said, all business now. "I'm dismissing the charges. Not because of the language business. Like I said, I think your client knows plenty enough English to understand the instructions to a field sobriety test" — she walked one fat hand in front of the other, in imitation of the toe-to-heel test — "and to consent to the Breathalyzer. I'm dismissing them because the officer never saw who was driving and just took your client's word that he was the driver. Mr. Rodríguez could have had a thousand reasons for claiming to be the driver and shouldering the blame. As we know, the truck belonged to one of the other fellas. That other fella has a revoked license, and maybe Mr. Rodríguez was trying to protect him. Or maybe Mr. Rodríguez thought he was the least drunk of the bunch and could beat the rap. Or maybe he was *so* drunk, he doesn't remember, like he said. As you know, we've subpoenaed the other two fellas to testify, but they're back in Mexico. So we'll never know. But I *do* know you rookie lawyers. You're gung ho. If I were to convict, you'd appeal. Say 'that old Judge Wallace, she'll get any Mexican that comes along.'"

"Are you dismissing the eluding charge too, Your Honor?" García asked quietly.

"Why, yes. That too. You may step down, Mr. Rodríguez."

García shook his bewildered client's hand. "That's it."

"¿Ya? ¿Todo?" the other Donaldo said.

"Yes. You're free to go."

His client stumbled to the elevator, eager to abandon the courthouse. García stepped out onto the third-floor balcony and inhaled the raw winter air. He felt like an idiot. He had made a mistake in calling Rodríguez to the stand and trying to maintain the fiction that his client understood no English. When the officer admitted he hadn't seen who was behind the wheel, why hadn't he changed his strategy and simply nailed the arresting officer on the identification problem? Even the most callow lawyer knew it was risky to call your client to the stand.

So why had he done it? Was it just because he had prepared a nice closing, one contingent upon Rodríguez's testifying to his inability to understand English, and was loath to give it up? And wasn't this inflexibility, this inability or unwillingness to change course, somehow the converse of his indecisiveness?

His closing, to be sure, had been well thought out. He would have maintained that his client's consent to the breath test had been the "fruit of the poisoned tree," since Mr. Rodríguez couldn't possibly understand the consent act in English. And from there he would have gone on to underscore not only the language gap but the cultural one as well, using information he'd gleaned from newspapers and books — the fact that in Mexico driving while intoxicated is not taken as seriously as it is here, and the police there are so notoriously corrupt that, innocent or otherwise, one would always seek to elude them. "None of which, Your Honor, is an excuse for not observing the law in this country — ignorance is never an excuse — I offer it only to show how much less egregious my client's actions were than they might otherwise appear," he would have said.

But there was something else that bothered him about his decision to go through with Mr. Rodríguez's testimony, something that made him feel dirty and deflated, and now he breathed the fresh air deeply in an effort to restore himself. It occurred to him that there had been something terribly self-serving in putting the alcoholic Mexican on the stand — something having to do with wanting to contrast himself, the slender, clearheaded Hispano attorney in a nailhead suit, with this disheveled, watery-eyed Mexican. Show people — the judge, the prosecutors, the cops, the clerk, the spectators — what a world of difference there was between these two tocayos, these two men of the same race and name.

And it occurred to him now that his need to show that difference stemmed from the fact that the PD's office had assigned him this case because everyone assumed there would exist a preternatural understanding between these two Latins, just as they assumed, erroneously, that García knew at least some Spanish. García closed his eyes at the thought that he had risked losing the case just to prove them wrong.

But he hadn't lost the case, and that, in the end, was what counted. That's what his colleagues would tell him. He could already feel their slaps on his back when he returned to the office. He'd won his first trial. It was a tradition at the office to have a little celebration when a PD won his or her first trial, go out for a couple of drinks at Toby's Tavern around the corner.

He couldn't go back to the office quite yet, though. There was something else he had to deal with, something unpleasant, also having to do with the trial, in some tangential way. Then he remembered, because he was staring straight at the yellow Brake Time sign on the street below. His car.

Bill Johnson sat on a stool amid the Brake Time tire display, squeezing his thumb slowly in a monkey wrench.

"You win?" he said when García walked in.

"I'm not sure you'd call it winning."

"You get your man off?"

"Yes."

"That's winning."

Bill squeezed the jaws tighter. His thumb turned fat and purple.

"Well," he said, "you didn't call."

"No," said García. "I didn't."

"Too busy helping the drunks walk free. Get them back behind the wheel."

García said nothing.

"We went ahead and did the work," said Johnson, sliding off the stool and tossing the wrench into a box. He went behind the counter and handed García the bill, the ignition key punched savagely through the middle of it, dangling.

García was braced for a big bill, but this was nearly five hundred dollars.

"What kind of brakes did you say they were?"

"The best in the business. Always go for the best. Just like if you were accused of a crime, say, driving drunk and slaughtering somebody on the road, you'd want the best defense, right? Well, around here you need the best brakes, to try to avoid all those goddamned, shit-faced, drunken sons a —"

García wrote out a check, without looking up. He hoped

there was enough in his account to cover it. He drove off the lot, touching the brakes at the intersection. They gripped like vises.

He parked in front of the public defenders' offices next to the courthouse and was about to feed the meter when he heard a voice.

"¡Tocayo!" It was Mr. Rodríguez. His breath was pungent with fresh courage. Mint, like the peppermint García had given him before the trial, but now laced with alcohol. Schnapps. He jabbered something in slurred Spanish.

"Maybe you forgot, Mr. Rodríguez. I don't speak Spanish." He felt simultaneously embarrassed and hopeful that the group of PDs standing around the entrance, smoking, had heard him.

"No, I just say thanks. You are the best, licenciado." He grabbed García's hand and forearm and pumped. His grip was sandpaper rough, his fingers deeply stained, as if they still bore the ink of his booking.

"Mr. Rodríguez," said García, extracting his hand, "do you need a ride somewhere?" García did not particularly relish the thought that Rodríguez might be headed to Toby's Tavern, the same bar to which García's colleagues would inevitably drag him, following tradition, to toast his first triumph at trial.

"I got a friend. He come for me."

"I'll take you where you want to go, Mr. Rodríguez. I've got a real good car." He patted its top. "It's got great brakes."

"No, no, no problem. My friend come here. I just call." He showed García a phone number penned in blue on his wrist, faded as an old prison tattoo. "I call, he come downtown. You got a quarter?"

"Well, as a matter of fact, I do." He handed Rodríguez the quarter, the famous quarter that he hadn't used to make his own call, and was about to put in the parking meter.

"Mr. Rodríguez," he said, as the man started toward the

phone booth in front of the courthouse. "Don't drink and drive. Right, Mr. Rodríguez? And don't let your friend drink and drive."

"Oh, no," said Rodríguez, shaking the coin happily in his fist.

García, his shoulders heavy, headed into the office, and to the celebration of his victory.

Careful

Jason Jefferson and a Hispanic guy were crossing the icy walk-way to the high school cafeteria one February day when the guy slipped, doing a funny little dance on the ice before he grabbed onto the railing, one arm and one leg flung out, like a ballerina. "Hey, cuiao," Jason said with a laugh, and caught, from the corner of his eye, the guy's look of alarm. Jason didn't know the guy, and he continued on to the cafeteria and got lost in the crowd.

Jason hadn't made any friends yet at his Colorado high school, having just transferred from out of state. The new school wasn't as big as his old one in Kansas, but it had a lot more Hispanics. He was taking Spanish and had learned a few useful words already, including this one, cuiao, which meant "be careful" or "watch out." It was spelled cuidado, and though his textbook said it was pronounced *kwee-dah-doh,* Mr.

Chávez, his teacher, said native speakers often didn't pro-
nounce the *d*'s. Jason liked that vowel-rich flow: cuiao.

The guy who had slipped on the ice and whom Jason had
said cuiao to wasn't in any of Jason's classes, but Jason had
noticed him around campus. He had what Jason called charisma. This was a quality that Jason couldn't quite define but
that he always recognized when he saw it. This guy's charisma
had something to do with his high cheekbones and his wavy
hair the color of red granite and his dark, slanted eyes. He had
a piratelike gold tooth in the deepness of his mouth, which
Jason once glimpsed in the cafeteria line when the guy tossed
his head back and laughed.

Jason now regretted having spoken to the guy, because of the
way the guy looked at him now across the cafeteria or as he
came down the halls. It was an unblinking look that carried
equal measures of curiosity and hostility, plus a glimmer of
something else, which, like the concept of charisma, Jason
didn't know exactly how to define. It was a look that made
Jason's testicles squirm. Jason wanted to talk to the guy, but he
couldn't bring himself to do it, even though he had mentally
rehearsed a dozen different indirect apologies for laughing at
him and saying "cuiao" when he had slipped on the ice.

Mr. Chávez cemented Jason's regret when he lectured the
class one day on the defensiveness a lot of Hispanic Americans
felt about the Spanish language, historically so maligned by the
Anglos who colonized the Southwest.

Jason raised his hand. "Like, if you're walking along and you
see this patch of ice and you point it out to a Spanish guy who's
walking along too and say, 'Cuiao,' he might get pissed?"

"He might indeed take umbrage — get pissed, as you so ele-
gantly put it, Jason — if he perceives you're somehow taunting
him, yes. Now that we're on the subject, one of the most common ways to say 'look out' in Mexico is 'aguas,' waters, which
dates from the days when people used to throw the contents of

their bedpans out into the street. And another very Mexican way of saying 'watch it' or 'keep your eye peeled' is 'abusado,' which is a corruption of 'aguzado,' which means 'sharp.' Abusado, in any other context means, of course, abused or misused."

"Oo-kay, let's see if we got today's lesson straight," said Earl Eastman, who sat in front of Jason. "If you see a patch of frozen piss in the street from somebody who's emptied a bedpan then you should warn people to get sharp, which is not to be confused with telling them to abuse themselves. Whatever."

Earl was smart and funny, and he, too, had charisma. Jason started hanging around him. The Hispanics called Earl a "stomper" because he dressed like a cowboy, hat and all, though he wasn't a cowboy. The Hispanics were leery of Anglo stompers. Stompers were "de cuidado": dangerous. It did not hurt at all to be associated with Earl, Jason thought, given the strange looks the granite-haired Hispanic guy kept giving him.

Earl had a drab little girlfriend named Roxy. Roxy had purplish circles under her eyes and a way of clinging to him like a skinny cat. Sometimes the three of them would go in Jason's pickup to the Burger Bowl for lunch, Jason insisting on riding in the back even when it was cold, because he sensed Roxy didn't really want him up front, and even if she did, he'd have felt uncomfortable sitting up there while she snuggled up and clung to Earl.

One lunch hour, after they had come back from the Burger Bowl and were getting out of the pickup, Jason heard Roxy ask Earl something in her mewling way and Earl replied, very clearly, "You bitch." There hadn't been the hint of an argument at the Burger Bowl to predict this, and Earl's words astonished Jason. Earl slammed his door and he and Roxy started walking in opposite directions, while Jason sat in the bed of the pickup and watched Roxy, then Earl, then Roxy. Roxy glanced back and saw Jason watching her and an expression between puzzled and annoyed crossed her face, and then she waved in that limp, halfhearted way she always waved to him and continued on her way.

Then Earl shouted, "Yo, buddy, gonna sit back there all day?" Jason jumped down and caught up with him, and they walked in silence to their class, Jason with a bounce in his step. Earl's girlfriend was a bitch and Jason was his buddy and it was a fine, sunny spring day.

That night, naked in bed, Jason thought about Earl and the coming warm weather and the things they might do together. They could go camping and fishing, and go to the rodeo, just the two of them, if indeed this falling-out between Earl and Roxy was permanent, as he hoped. And there did seem to be something serious and irreparable about that matter-of-fact, publicly spoken "You bitch." Roxy's little halfhearted wave to Jason seemed to him to say: "I know you and I aren't friends, Jason, but could you help me and Earl. . . . No, I guess not, I guess it's over."

"Bitch," what a word. Guys called each other bitch now, especially the school's two black dudes, and some of the cholos. The first time he had heard a guy call another guy bitch happened a few days after he had enrolled in this school, in the wooded area behind the cafeteria that people called the pines. Mark, a rat-tailed Anglo dude from one of Jason's classes, tried to bum a cigarette off a cholo and the cholo said, "Get your own, bitch," and Mark said something back to him in Spanish. The fight was quick. In a few seconds the cholo had Mark turned around and pinned against a ponderosa. He wrapped Mark's rat-tail in his fist and mashed his face into the trunk of the tree. He braced his knees against the back of Mark's legs and murmured something into his ear, like a lover. The cholo murmured into Mark's ear for a long time, or so it seemed to Jason, but then time had slowed for Jason, and the cloudless blue sky seemed to grow darker, and the sunlight deeper, more golden, illuminating the scene with a kind of frozen intensity. The cholo's tongue flashed into Mark's ear and Mark tensed and the cholo's friends gave uneasy little laughs. Eventually the cholo let Mark go, and Mark stumbled off, rubbing his ear, the jeers of the cholo's friends at his back.

Jason, lying in bed in the dark, held a piece of ponderosa bark to his nose and stroked his erection. Ponderosa bark smelled like butterscotch, and he imagined butterscotch was what Mark had smelled when the cholo pushed his face into the trunk and whispered into his ear. Jason dug his fingernail into the bark and peeled away its jigsaw layers to release the scent. "Bitch," he gasped when he came.

He tossed the piece of bark away and lay staring at the ceiling. He wondered how loud he had said "bitch" and if his parents in the next room had heard it. Then, in that clearness of mind that always accompanied his shame, it dawned on him that Earl had not said "you bitch" to Roxy at all. What he had said was "you betcha." She had asked him something like, "Are you coming over tonight, Earl?" and he had replied, "You betcha." Jason's realization of his mistake fell on him like a weight from the darkness and punched a hiccupping, pained laugh from his chest.

Jason did not hang with Earl and Roxy as much after that, and they did not seem to miss him. When he did hang with them, it was usually because he felt the Hispanic guy, the guy who had slipped on the ice, watching him in his solitude. When the feeling that the guy was watching him got too intense, Jason went to Earl and Roxy and stuck around them even when they ignored him. He didn't think he was afraid of the Hispanic guy, exactly. The guy didn't seem to belong to a ganga or clicka or have any friends he had to prove anything to, and he didn't swagger or act macho. Still, whenever he saw the guy watching him in that penetrating way, Jason's mouth went dry.

One afternoon, Roxy and Earl decided to cut class and go to the pines and smoke a blunt. Jason, who had twice that day caught the Hispanic guy looking at him, invited himself along.

It would be the first time he had gone into the pines since he'd seen the cholo beat up Mark there, but with Earl it felt safe to go there. In fact, it would be good for the Hispanic guy, in case he was still watching, to see that Jason and his friends were the kind of unafraid people who went to the pines to smoke dope.

The pines were abandoned that afternoon, the only sound the hissing of the warm May breeze through their long needles. Earl and Roxy and Jason sat on a ponderosa's rough roots, and Earl lit the blunt. Jason believed this might be the same tree the cholo had pinned Mark against, though he couldn't be sure. After a couple of hits, Roxy said she didn't want anymore, and Earl gingerly snuffed the roach out on the bark of the root. A smell of scorched butterscotch rose in the air.

Roxy unbuttoned her shirt and lay in the bright sun, her black halter top like a shadow thrown across her scrawny breasts. After a moment she said something in a low voice to Earl and they both got up. Jason got up too.

"Not him," Roxy murmured.

"We're gonna take off, now, dude," Earl told Jason. And then they were gone, headed up the creek and to those isolated spots where couples sometimes went for privacy.

Jason sat back down. He was stoned, with a floating feeling. He noticed that Earl had forgotten to take the roach with him: it lay on the ponderosa root. He closed his eyes and rested his head against the tree's sunlit trunk and smelled the scent of butterscotch. He got hard and squeezed himself through his jeans, and when he opened his eyes again the sunlight had that deep, golden quality. He told himself he shouldn't be in the pines alone, but he made no effort to move. Then he saw the Hispanic guy, the guy who had slipped on the ice, leaning against a nearby tree.

"Got a cigarette?" the guy asked.

The sunlight turned a shade darker. Jason drew himself into the crotch of roots. His mouth, already dry from the dope, went to stone. He shook his head.

The guy pushed himself away from his tree and went to where Jason sat. He picked up the roach, struck a kitchen match against the bark, and lit it. He loomed above Jason. He took a slow hit, letting the smoke swirl around in his open mouth before inhaling. Jason saw the gold pirate tooth glimmer behind the silver swirls of smoke.

Then the guy squatted, his jeans drawing in a heart shape across his buttocks and the heels of his scuffed harness boots sinking into the soft pine needles. The toe of one of his boots touched Jason's thigh. He passed the roach to Jason.

"A funny cigarette," the guy said. "A queer cigarette."

Then the guy said, "Hey. Why did you call me queer?"

Jason felt the bark dig into his back. "What?" he whispered.

"When I slipped on the ice. Why did you say, 'Hey, queer'?"

Jason swallowed hard. "No, man," he said. "I didn't say queer. I said cuiao. Spanish, you know, for 'look out.'"

"Cuiao?"

"Yeah."

"Like, 'hey, cuiao, ése?'"

"Yeah," said Jason. "Like, careful."

The guy gazed at Jason and then beyond him, into the woods.

"Yeah. I figured I heard wrong. I figured a guy wouldn't just come up to me and say, 'Hey, queer.' Unless he was queer in the head."

"No, man."

The guy laughed a low laugh, and Jason gave his hiccupping one. "I guess it's like my friend," said Jason, jerking his thumb in the direction of the creek. "I thought he said 'You bitch' to his girlfriend, but what he said was 'You betcha.'"

This time the guy laughed his big laugh, the one with his head thrown back, gold tooth gleaming. Jason felt the flow return to his blood then. The sunlight mellowed in its richness.

The guy relit the cold roach and they passed it back and forth. Even when it was a tiny nub, they kept passing it, their stained fingers touching, negotiating. When Jason could no longer take it, the guy settled beside him and held it up to his lips. Jason inhaled, but there was no more smoke, just the warm smell of the guy's fingers mixed with the scent of the ponderosa trunks baking in the afternoon heat.

They sat in silence for a long time. The guy crossed his legs, and when his knee touched Jason's, neither of them shifted to break the contact. Finally Jason spoke, his voice husky and distant in his ears: "So what would you do if, you know, I'd really said, 'Hey, queer'?"

The guy studied him, his pupils large, his bronze cheekbones prickled with a flush. Then he leaned over, his knee brushing Jason's thigh, and whispered softly into his ear: "I'd say, 'You bitch.'"

Desiring Desire

Beth is prepping masa for tamales when the phone rings. It's Josh. She's transported to the previous summer, to the day he called excitedly to report he'd found a source for fresh banana leaves for wrapping the tamales. As her helper at her small Santa Fe catering business, he had made many such discoveries. Sometimes they were off the wall: he once ordered two dozen crocus bulbs so they could grow their own saffron, not realizing how many hundreds it would take to yield enough of the spice to flavor more than just a few paellas. But the banana leaves were wonderful. So in that instant before she realizes this is *this* summer, not last, and before she registers the strange new gravity in his voice, she feels a glad surge in her heart.

"I just got in from Wyoming," he says. "I was wondering if I could see you."

The mention of Wyoming jerks her to the recollection of another, less delightful, call from him. It had come last winter, late at night, the snow swirling. It was the last she had heard from him, before today. He was calling from Cheyenne to tell her, again excitedly, that something very, very good had happened to him, that he couldn't get into it now, but that it was a very, very good thing and that he would give her the details later. He sounded manic, a little drunk maybe. She really didn't want to know about his good thing, because she suspected it involved a woman. She told him it was too late to be calling her, and he apologized and said he would call back some other time. He never did.

Now here he is, back in Santa Fe, wanting to "see" her. What does it mean, to "see" somebody, or more to the point, what does it mean for him to want to see her? She's three years older than he, thirty, she has her own steady little business, and she really isn't interested in hearing about his adventures. Besides, she's a mess, her hair dangling in sweaty strands down her neck from under the baseball cap she wears when she cooks, her jeans and apron doing nothing to hide the weight she's put on in the last year.

"I'm kind of busy, Josh," she says. She rolls the drying masa into little balls between her fingers. When he doesn't reply, she says, "Where are you?"

"On the plaza. I've been on the road two days. I've been in some trouble."

"Are you all right?"

"Yeah, yeah. I just need somebody to talk to, is all."

She can't remember anyone ever saying to her, "I'm in trouble." She doesn't know the kind of people that get into trouble, and even fewer who might confide their troubles to her. In Santa Fe, at least among the comfortable New Age people she deals with in her catering business, one is more likely to hear someone admit he or she is a visiting alien from the Pleiades than confess to any earthly concerns. And now here's a man, a man of whom she had been quite fond, coming to her out of nowhere with his problems.

"Well, if you need to talk . . ."

"Okay, I'll come on by," he says, and hangs up.

She considers getting out of her work clothes and doing something with her hair, but decides against it. It really isn't her style to change her appearance for anybody. In that way, she remains a certain kind of St. John's College woman, defiantly indifferent to appearance. The outer has nothing to do with one's essence, one's *eidos*. Josh, on the other hand, had gone through a dandy stage at the college, not to mention a party stage — she had always been amazed, impressed, at how prepared he was at seminar, and wondered how he found the time to do the reading. He had dropped out after sophomore year to bum around the world, but she finished the four years of the Great Books program without interruption, and stayed on in Santa Fe, working as a sous chef at Chez Nous before forming her own catering business.

Last summer, she ran into him by chance. He'd just blown into town. She hadn't seen him for five years. He said he'd worked at no fewer than twelve restaurants all over Europe. Half jokingly, she asked if he wanted to work for her, and to her surprise he said he'd like that. He came to her kitchen nearly every weekday morning, brimming with energy and ideas. Their relationship developed along playfully platonic lines. When they weren't talking about food, they engaged in ironic debate about life's Big Questions — the kind of debates they had occasionally had at St. John's, as informal continuations of their seminars. He didn't reveal much about his private life, though she knew he was "seeing" at least one woman. Beth, who not long before had broken up with a boyfriend, and who now spent her free time dabbling in Buddhism and other Eastern religions, took a cynical view of relationships. As the

Buddha's second Truth put it, the passions were life's greatest trap. In her experience — and her confession embarrassed her as soon as it came out of her mouth — once you expressed your desire for a man, he no longer desired you. So unless you are able to achieve Nirvana — the overcoming of desire altogether — which she certainly hadn't, you should desire only your own desire, and leave it at that. "Ah, I think I hear the mysterious sound of one hand clapping," he had said. "Whereas two people desiring each other, that's just the shallow smacking of two."

In the fall, when the busy summer season had wound down, he took off again on his travels, though he never mentioned Wyoming as a destination. She hadn't realized how much she would miss him.

Nor had she imagined how much a man's appearance could change in a year. He had always been wiry, but now, as he reaches his long arm around to unlatch her gate, she sees he is downright gaunt. He wears a droopy moustache, which makes him seem even thinner. He has a two-day beard. He looks like the kind of man you might find in the back of a Greyhound bus, cradling a bottle of wine. Indeed, the Greyhound is what he's taken from Wyoming, he tells her. He smells strong, but of sweat, not of alcohol. It's kind of pleasant, like cumin.

He takes off his Western hat and leans his skinny rump against the kitchen sink and his face into his hands. "Oh, man." He looks at her with road-reddened eyes and asks how things are going with her, the catering business. Same old, same old, she says. She hires serving staff from the same temp agency, and a man helps her out in the kitchen occasionally — gay, of course, like most of the men in Santa Fe, it would appear. Then she asks him about himself.

"The short and skinny of it? Tomorrow morning by eight I've got to turn myself in to the Laramie County, Wyoming, jail."

Beth has never known a man who has been to jail, or at least not well enough that he would have told her about it.

"What for?" she says, trying not to show her dismay.

"It's complicated. I violated probation. They put me on probation for fighting with a guy, and one of the conditions was that I not see the woman we were fighting over. Well, screw that. I can't believe I actually have to do time. Her dad's well connected up there, and he's after my ass. And then there's the rival, the guy the dad *does* like. A rich little prick. Now I hear they're getting married." Josh shakes his head and gives a little laugh. "Like two bucks in rutting season, we were."

"So it had to do with the good thing," Beth says.

"Good thing?"

"The good thing you called me about from Cheyenne."

"Oh. Yeah. Not a good thing, though. Not a good thing at all."

"Is it long? The sentence, I mean."

"Ninety days. Half that with good time. But if I don't show tomorrow, I guess it could get a lot worse. At the hearing, the judge said he'd give me a few days to get my affairs in order before I had to report to do my time, but he ordered me not to leave the county. The problem was, I didn't know anybody in the whole state that I could really talk to. And that's what getting my affairs in order means to me: somebody I can talk to, help me get my head together."

That he has traveled hundreds of miles to talk to her, in defiance of a judge's orders, makes Beth feel weak. What makes him think she'll be able to advise him? The smell of the tamales steaming in their banana leaves reminds her of that happy summer they worked together in this kitchen; but this slightly rancid sweat of his belongs to the man she doesn't know. A man who can become obsessed over a woman, fight over her, and go to jail for it. She has never thought much about jail, but it must be awful to be locked up in a small, hot space, with just your regrets and your longings and your conscience to torment you.

"It's too hot in this little kitchen," she says. "Let's sit outside, okay? Would you like something to eat or drink? Coffee, a croissant?"

They sit at a table of crazed Mexican tile, under the tree of heaven. The pink flagstones of her small patio are buckled from the tree's roots, and their chairs rest at angles. The croissants, which have two separate layers of cream filling between the puff pastry, are her own recent invention. He takes a bite of one, looks at its insides. "Oh, that's good," he says.

"Josh," Beth says quietly. "Was there a lot of violence?"

"Violence? I shoved the guy once, that's it. Did you know that's assault and battery? You point at a guy, that's an assault. Touch him with the finger, there's your battery. Six months' probation was the initial sentence, with the aforementioned condition that I have no contact with her. Her father had private detectives watching me, can you believe it?"

"She must be some precious creature, to have so many males looking after her."

"It's so fucking ridiculous. I swear to God, I don't even remember what the woman looks like. I just thought of her as ideal."

"The ideal woman. No wonder you don't remember."

"Okay, she had dark eyebrows and blond hair. That's a prerequisite."

"I'll try to remember that. The ideal woman has dark eyebrows and blond hair."

"All right, so I'm a jerk. So sue me. Better, lock me up."

He leans back in his chair and closes his bloodshot eyes to the sun. The light glinting whitely off his stubble makes him look old.

"Desire of desire," he says after a while, his eyes still shut. "That's the ticket. To desire desire for itself alone."

She plays along, pretending as if they hadn't had this conversation last summer. "Ticket to what?"

"To Nirvana!"

"So you're into Zen now, Joshua?"

In their debates back then, he had maintained that Buddhism was too "passive" for him. He said he was too much an "active Westerner" for Eastern religions. She wonders if he's seen her new Zen garden in the corner, whose pale pebbles she slowly, ritually rakes every morning before starting her day.

"Yeah, I'm the Buddha incarnate," he says, patting his non-existent belly.

She smiles. Their debates on the Big Questions have always had this ironic tenor, as if they are leery of getting bogged down in seriousness. Seriousness is marshy ground in which one can too easily flounder, but the irony in their repartee keeps them buoyant.

"Actually, I think it was Nietzsche who said it," he says. "'In the end, all we really desire is our own desire.' All you have to do is let it envelop you, like layers of fat . . ."

The way he catches himself annoys her.

"It's pathetic," she says, with a vehemence that surprises her. "It's self-defeating. Not to mention totally un-Zen. Putting desire at one remove like that — that's not the way to Nirvana, that's double ignorance."

He cracks his eyes a slit to look at her. A breeze moves the branches of the tree of heaven, and a sliver of bright sunlight reflects off the plate of pastries and slices over his face.

"I don't know. I find people who truly just desire their own desire rather attractive."

"Is that true of your ideal woman, too, Josh? Does she find it attractive? Is that what you plan to do, sit in your cell, desiring your own desire, hoping she'll come break you out?"

Joshua laughs. "Now *that* would be a very un-Zenlike hope, wouldn't it? As you used to say, Zen isn't goal-oriented, right? It would be hypocritical to use the desire of your own desire to attract the *true* object of your desire. Still, I don't think it's exactly self-defeating. It's more like self-fulfilling. I mean, if desiring your own desire fails to make others desire you, then all it truly leaves you to fall back on is your own desire."

"You know what it is?" she says. "It's all self-pity. That's all it is."

She gets up brusquely from the table and goes to check the tamales. Anger is a useless emotion, she knows that. Still, she feels it — an anger deriving (she knows this too, at least) from her own confusion. What are they talking about? *Who* are they talking about? In an oblique way, aren't they talking about her, Beth?

Over the long summer they had cooked together, every time he brushed against her in that small kitchen it was as if he'd brushed something inside her. And while that thing recoiled further within her, seeking protection, the kitchen expanded, became limitless in its space and possibility. After he left Santa Fe, the thing remained deep inside her, covered over by her very desire of it, "like layers of fat," as he has untactfully put it. Is he implying that he knows she's drawn to him, that he knows she's been unable to renounce her desire? If so, then his presumption is breathtaking in its arrogance.

Beth snatches off the lid of the tamale steamer. She brings her face too close to it, and the steam, carrying with it the concentrated aroma of cooking banana leaves that reminds her so of the previous summer, blasts her. She bucks back, knocking a copper kettle from its hook. It falls with a terrific clatter. Josh appears instantly in the kitchen.

"I'm all right," she says. "Dammit, I'm always getting scalded or burned these days."

Josh swoops the kettle up before it finishes spinning on its perfectly balanced edge, and eases it noiselessly back on its hook. He is as smooth-moving a man as she's ever seen, and this fluidness is infectious. When she was working with him, she got hurt a lot less.

She has a week-old burn on her forearm, long and bright as a worm, and he looks at it now. Afraid he might reach out to touch it, she turns away and pretends to adjust the flame under the burner. She had always become more efficient and keen to her tasks when working close to him. Maybe this also was why she got hurt less — his presence, rather than flustering her, forced her to concentrate on her work.

"How many more tamales do you have to make?" he asks.

"Five dozen, at least."

"If I can get cleaned up first," he says, "I'll help."

The water running in the shower sounds strange to her from the kitchen, and she realizes she's never heard anyone bathe in her place, save herself. It's disconcerting, in the same way it was disconcerting when Josh first came to work for her and she discovered apples in the hydrator or the garlic press resting in the bowl of garlic — sensible places, but ones that had never occurred to her. Most disconcerting about it is her disconcertation itself — it tells her she's been alone too long.

They sit down at the long kitchen table to make the tamales. He's fresh now, his wet hair slicked back, cheeks shaven and moustache smoothed, even his brown eyes clearer — like a cunning pup walrus popped up from the deep. The easy, efficient manner with which he builds the tamales, folding the filling into them and wrapping the sleek banana leaves expertly around them, soothes her. Maybe she has read too much into their conversation on the patio; maybe it is her ego putting herself at the center of it. Next she'll be believing he's been secretly in love with her all along, and took off to Wyoming in desperation, searching for the love she'd refused to show him.

"Tamale and tamale and tamale," Josh says. "Life creeps in this petty pace from day to day. . . . Isn't that Shakespeare?"

Beth gives a raucous shout of laughter. Josh breaks her up more than any man she's ever known. She can feel the fat on her belly jiggle.

"Let's build another couple dozen," she says when she's recovered. "There's a cooked roast in foil in the refrigerator behind you."

Josh slices meat from the roast. Beth says, "Do you know the story about the Buddhist butcher?"

"Aren't Buddhists vegetarians?"

"Well, this one wasn't. Actually, he was a monk, a Buddhist monk. Yeah, that's the ticket."

"You're crazy," says Josh. "Okay, so tell me about the Buddhist butcher monk."

"Well, one day an apprentice came to him to learn the meat-cutting trade. The monk told him he'd have to sharpen his knife every hour. After he became an expert, he'd have to sharpen it only once a day, then once a week. 'Now, me,' said the monk, 'I don't sharpen mine anymore at all.' 'How's that, Master?' said the apprentice. 'Well,' said the monk, 'whereas you cut the meat, I pass my knife through the spaces within the meat.'"

She half expects Josh to say something sarcastic, as he would have in the old days, but he says, "So how'm I cutting it?"

"You're doing fine," Beth replies. "But you're no monk."

"Now there's a Noble Truth," he says. "I'm no monk."

A cicada's buzz splits the air. It lives somewhere in the tree of heaven, and from mid-June it always begins its song about now, one o'clock. You can practically set your clock by it.

"Josh," she says suddenly, "when did you say you had to, you know, go back?" She feels bad about mentioning it, but it occurs to her that the day is getting on and Wyoming is a long way away.

"Check-in time at the inn is 8:00 A.M. tomorrow. Thanks for reminding me."

He piles the shredded pork carefully at one end of the scarred cutting board.

"But how far is Cheyenne? How are you going to get there?"

"Goddammit to hell," he says, "I don't know."

His face is pale and tight now, and she turns away. She doesn't like seeing him like this.

"Josh, what happens if you don't go back?"

"I don't know. I guess they put out a warrant. The bail bondsmen go looking for you. The bounty hunters."

"Is that really what they call them? Bounty hunters?"

"The bondsmen pay them a percentage to find you. They figure that's better than forfeiting the whole bond to the court."

Jail, Beth thinks, is not a good place. Men get beat up there. They get raped. They get diseases. In Josh's case, isn't it better, for everyone involved, that he be here, hundreds of miles from the source of his troubles? What sense does it make for him to go back there? Has jail ever helped anyone?

"Does anyone know you're here?" she says in a whisper, as if someone else could hear them.

"Nope."

"You never told anyone in Wyoming that you had worked for a caterer in Santa Fe? You never told them my name?"

"Not a soul."

This news relieves and wounds her at the same time. She steps out to the patio to be alone with her thoughts. The cicada's buzz is loud, steady. Black afternoon clouds boil over the mountains, but it's sunny yet here, and still. She goes to the Zen garden and kneels beside it. So he had told no one. Told no one he'd left behind a good thing in Santa Fe, an ideal but unapproachable woman that he would someday go back to after he'd sown his wild oats. Nothing like that. Instead, he's come here precisely because he's told no one, because his silence makes this a good place to hide. A cynical person might say he was just using her for protection, and she in turn had a captive in him.

But it didn't have to be that way. It didn't have to be that way at all. That cynical person also thought of Buddhism as endless wheels of miserable desire and resistance to desire. But in fact, Zen taught you to be fully present to a world full of risk and possibility. To defeat fear. True, it meant the fear of loneliness, among other fears. But didn't it also mean the fear of desiring the object of desire?

Among the pebbles of the garden lies the transparent, molted skin of a cicada. Perhaps it was shed by the one crying now in the tree. It is perfectly formed, except for the split down the middle; even the skin of the eyes is intact. The storm clouds piling toward them, and the winds that too easily snap the tree's brittle branches, will soon hush the creature's noise. And in another month autumn will be here, and the cicada will disappear for good, leaving only the sparse clicking of the katy-dids, and then the winter will silence them, too. She reminds herself that the seasons are only a reflection of the samsara, the eternal cycle of birth, suffering, death, and rebirth, the dread of which can be overcome by True Practice. But today she can't help but dread the thought of another cold winter alone; her desire right now, as she feels the warmth around her, as she catches a tropical whiff of steaming banana leaves from the kitchen where Josh sits, is that the summer stay, forever.

Pickup

Lucha caught up with me at the motel in Big Spring. Rajiv — Ray, as he preferred us gringos to call him — knocked timidly on my door and said the "gentleman" had a phone call. Gentleman. Man or woman, I asked. Lady, he said. Well, it must be Lu, I thought. I guess I made it easy enough for her to track me down by putting the motels on my credit card, the bill for which goes to our Austin address.

A blast of hot air and curry smacked me as I entered the office and picked up the cracked black receiver.

"Now, look," said Lucha, "that truck may be in both our names, but I've made most of the payments on it, so you just roll it right on back here to Austin so we can put it up for sale. I mean it, now."

Lucha was a mexicana, but she could talk like a tough White lady. Her name meant "struggle," which I thought was a pretty funny name, but I guess it's common enough in Mexico. From her tone right now, I could tell she truly meant she just wanted the pickup back, and not me. But how was I going to start a new life without a vehicle, especially out here in West Texas? That brand-new Ford could take me anywhere I liked across these sprawling counties, which my road map reminds me are huge and empty compared to East Texas counties. I mean, I'm from these parts, originally, but I had forgotten how empty and lonesome it can be out here. In fact, the county map of Texas looks disturbingly like a map I once saw of what the curved universe might look like, a kind of funnel-shaped business with the small grids jammed at one end and opening to nothingness at the other. Well, as they say, West Texas ain't the end of the world, but you can see it from here.

"I don't know, Lu," I said. "I could try to sell it out here and send you the money."

"No, uh-uh. I want it here." Lu didn't trust me.

We breathed at one another for a while. Then she said, "If it helps you any, he still can't make bail. And in case you're further interested, she's still in the hospital."

"She" was Ronnie. "He" was Ronnie's husband.

I didn't know what to say. What could I say? So there was another silence, upon which she just said, "Oh, just get the damn truck over here and let's settle it, want to?" and hung up.

I stared down at the postcards under the counter glass, postcards of the motel, sky the bluest blue, sign — WESTERN WINDS — the reddest red, and the parking lot full of, what else, pickups. Ray was in the back, gobbling rice and gabbing happily with his wife and kids.

Lucha and I had had a happy home ourselves until my thing with Ronnie, which culminated in Ronnie's old man catching her waiting for me in the pickup at the Blue Bell Court and putting her in intensive care. Ronnie and I had known each other only a couple weeks. I had picked her up at a funky little northside honky-tonk called the Outhouse. I would have taken her to a place more hidden than the Blue Bell, which was kind of too near both our homes for proper discretion, but her husband, a trucker and true bubba, was supposedly still on his run, and Lu was across town waiting tables, so we figured the Blue Bell would be safe enough. We pulled into the parking lot, and I told Ronnie I'd be right back with the room key and some Shiner. I walked over to the icehouse next door, and from there I saw her old man's rig roll by, snort to an almost jackknife stop, and back wildly into the Blue Bell lot. I got the cashier to call the police right away, and then I hid behind the icehouse Dumpster. I could hear the yelling and screaming and carrying on, and I have to confess I wet my pants. The cops came pretty quick, and then I went over. The cop took my statement. The next day a couple of ladies from Human Services, domestic violence branch or whatever, came to interview me at home, and that's how the cat got out of the bag and Lu learned about the whole thing.

Leaving the Western Winds the morning after Lucha's call, I'm having these thoughts: either I can keep being the full-fledged son of a bitch I've become and blow old Lu off and head up to Canada, say, like a draft dodger, or I can do the gentlemanly thing and drag myself back like a half-assed crawdad the way she's ordered. I'm thinking these things as I let the Ford's engine warm up a little bit before pulling out onto Highway 87. It's a cold December morning, the sky clotted with thin clouds like a cheap blanket. A blue norther complete with ice storms and all that good stuff is set to roll in this afternoon. Mist lies low on the fallow cotton fields, and there's no traffic on the road.

I truly do not know how I want to turn, left or right.

Until, that is, a Ford pickup identical to my own, minus the dents Ronnie's husband put in my door and hood, speeds by, headed southeast toward San Angelo. Same brand-new model, same color even, cherry red, piloted by a blonde. Her windows are fogged up, so she goes by in a blur.

I peel left and follow her, laying tread.

This is not a pleasant stretch of highway. The tumbleweeds lie piled up against the fences like skeletons, the air stinks of oil-field sulphur, and the only landmarks are those furious, weirdly disembodied orange flames flaring the gas off distant rigs. So I fall back a little, thinking it's a threatening thing to ride someone's tail on these end-of-the-world highways. Then I think, what the hell, that's all paranoia, and all because I watched *Road Warrior* and *Mad Max* on my motel HBO the other night. This wasn't some futuristic nightmare, this was West Texas circa 1990, where harshness and desolation bring people together, make strangers friendly. So I put my vehicle into overdrive — loved the transmission in that thing, I could picture its gears pristine and silver, bathed in their clear, cherry-gold tranny oil — and pass her, honking a howdy-do beep and putting my thumb and forefinger in an o as if to say what a fine vehicle she has — *we* have.

She doesn't respond, as I more than half expected she wouldn't. The men in these parts always give other drivers an index finger salute from the steering wheel, but the women never do. Doesn't mean they're hostile. When the women here are hostile, they'll let you know it; they'll give you the one-fingered salute, all right, but it's not the index finger.

I slow and she passes me, and then I pass her again, and like that. I detect a definite playfulness in the way she zips by, in the way her own overdrive kicks in just as she draws parallel to me. But I can't really get a good look at her; her windows are still steamed, and streaked on the outside with red hardscrabble dust. She remains a reddish ghost.

We sail right through San Angelo, but when we get to tiny Eden, she turns into the driveway of a low brick ranch house and pulls in behind the tight windbreak evergreens. It's a junky, bubba-ish kind of place, with Christmas lights draped half-heartedly over the evergreens and a chipped Styrofoam Santa looming over the roof. I hear her door slam, but I can't catch a glimpse of her. I cruise around the block one time, then head for my much-needed pit stop. I need gas, coffee, a pissoir for my weak bladder, and a chance to figure out my game plan.

The place is an old, weathered joint with a couple of Texaco pumps out front and a bunting on the railing reading, DEER STORAGE AND SMOKEHOUSE. HUNTERS WELCOME. Inside's a café, and the café is full of big-gutted ranchers and idle roustabouts lounging in broken-spring Naugahyde booths and chewing the fat in drawls that all the caffeine in Colombia can't speed up. Not that the sockwater coffee here is Colombian. After all, this is Concho County, not Austin. Lu, I recall with something like a pang of regret, had recently learned all about fine coffees and could make a kick-ass cup of Colombian, complete with the little rainbow bubbles on top.

"It'll be a minute before it drips through," says the scrawny waitress.

"I hope that's a New York minute," I say. "I got places to go, people to meet."

"She's on Texas time," says the character next to me, grinning through tobacco-stained teeth. He has a red pig face, squeenchy little eyes, and a Roadway gimme cap that pinches the bristly flesh above his ears.

I turn in my stool and keep my eye on the highway and my ear half on the conversations around me, the grunting about the cotton quota, the sheared shear pin, the bit that won't bite, the weather, always the damned weather, and I'm thinking, nope, I don't think I can live in West Texas ever again.

"Hey, buddy," I say suddenly to the bubba beside me, "see that red four-on-the-floor out there with the lake pipes?"

He turns and looks out at my pickup.

"Ever seen one like it?" I say.

"Can't say I have," he says. He's trying to humor me by agreeing that I have the only cherry-red Ford pickup in the world.

"Well," I say, "I'll have you know there's a pretty little lady somewhere around here driving one just like it, just frisky as a filly."

"Yeah?" says the bubba, turning a little bit redder, his eyes a little wetter, watching me.

"You wouldn't happen to know who that is, now, would you?"

"No," says the bubba slowly, "don't reckon I do." He's a little nervous now, not quite sure what I'm getting at.

Why do I do it? Lu says it has something to do with resentment, arrogance, something about my roots, my daddy, and, when she's really pissed, something about my mama. I don't know, I'm not a psychologist. All I know at the moment is that if I'm quick, I can make the move on this lady before these good folks ever know what hit 'em. I could park my pickup right in the driveway behind her hidden one and neighbors would think nothing of it, since they are identical. If she's alone, hot dog — I'd have one of her old man's beers and we'd do a quickie on the filthy shag, all in the time it would take this dimwit next to me here to figure it out and get word to him and by the time he came home, I'd be outta there.

And if her old man's already home, heck, we'd just talk trucks and have a friendly old time, marveling at coincidences and such, as the savage wind howls through the mesquite outside.

But I have to jettison this game plan, because just then I see her pull onto 87 and head east. "Gotta run!" I say, grabbing my coffee, scalding my fingers pleasantly. The chase is on again.

I follow her at my leisure, sockwater sloshing happily in its Styrofoam, radio playing songs like "All My Exes Live in Texas" and the one where the guy asks the girl to do "something insensitive" with him, "something we'll both regret."

After the town of Brady she takes 71, that Hill Country road that squiggles its way straight to Austin. The deejay announces that the norther is moving in quickly now. We run into sudden patches of fog thick as mattresses, and I see a couple of deer

bouncing stiff-legged and bewildered through the scrub. On-
ward through the fog, as old Oat Willie, the icon of Austin,
says.

At one point, I get far ahead of her and then pull over and try
to wave her down. She doesn't even slow, but I do believe I can
see a coy smile through the blur.

And so we go, flying over those hills like a couple of kids on
a roller coaster, that mysterious blond head swaying ahead of
me, past all those romantic-sounding towns, Marble Falls,
Spicewood, Bee Cave. Night is falling as we near Austin, the
rush-hour traffic is thickening, and the weather has made a
severe turn for the nastier, the frigid fog having become tiny
shards of ice. I'm thinking, Damn, I'm going to lose her, she's
going to get sucked into this icy night. My only recourse then
was going to be one of those slender-hope personal ads in the
Chronicle: "Followed you all the way from Big Spring, 12/15.
Lost you on I-35. Please contact," etc. Dammit, why did this
have to get difficult, as in real life? Why doesn't she make it
easy and take an exit?

I decide I have to pull abreast of her and motion for her to
take the next off ramp. It's going to be tough. The rush-hour
traffic is mean and tight, chunks of dull metal blasting through
the freezing rain. I can sense the warm minds inside thinking,
knowing, that everything will turn out fine if no one plays any
games, pulls any dumb stunts that will cause anyone else to
brake or swerve. When I begin to slalom through the traffic, it's
like a psychological wrench thrown into the works. The mood
of the drivers around me shifts from tense calm to open hostility: brights flash in my rearview mirror, a horn blares a long
warning. But I do manage finally to pull alongside her on the
right. I flash my lights, motion desperately for her to follow me
off the next exit ramp, my old familiar exit, the one to both the
Blue Bell and, in the other direction, Lu's and my place.

A giant tractor-trailer rig is on my tail now, bearing down on me angrily, pushing me forward as her lane slows. He's pissed. But I'm pissed too. After this long chase, this redneck is trying to blow my last chance at what would surely be a good thing. I slow. Okay, I brake. I go into a skid, but turn into it and correct. The rig makes a Jake-brake snort like a startled bull. I shoot off into my exit, glancing into the mirror to see the rig fishtail. Then it glides in a smooth, weird way into the fast lane, and that's all I see.

As I skid down the ramp, I enter the dream world of my own accident. An alert driver in the intersection below, and then another, try to scramble out of my way. I spin out of control and then come to a neat stop at the curb, as though I had parked there. One of the drivers lifts his hands and silently applauds, the other shakes his head in disgust and amazement, and both move cautiously on their way.

I sit there for a while, adrenaline numbing my hands and feet, a chemical smell in my nose. I roll down the window with dread and listen. Shouts come muffled through the crystalline air, I hear the slamming of car doors, the clang of metal to pavement. I don't stick around for the sirens.

Tires whining, I make my way home. I feel a moisture — I've wet my pants again. I get out, shaking. I slip and fall on the ice. The walkway is so icy and I'm so weak-kneed I have to crawl up to the house, up to where the lights glow warmly, dragging my balls. When I get to the porch I can smell the rich Colombian coffee, and I can smell gingerbread. When Lucha answers my knock she'll look at me and think I've been drinking, she'll have that look of contempt, and all I'll be able to say is, "I brought it to you, your truck, there it is. Will you let me in, will you please, please let me in?"

Spring

The doorbell rang like the tolling of church bells and doña Eulalia Martínez jumped out of her skin.

"¿Quién vive?" she almost cried out. "¿Quién vive?" That was something her late husband had always exclaimed when startled. He inevitably said it whenever the phone or the doorbell rang. Sudden noises alarmed him, but he had excellent vision in his one good eye. As a boy, he had been one of Pancho Villa's lookouts when Villa was hiding out in the cave, so good was that telescope eye.

She quickly slipped back into her skin, which at her age was loose-fitting anyway, and sneaked to the door. Who, this early in the morning? Surely not the Jehovahs? She rose on tiptoes and peered through the peephole (she had shrunk that much since it was installed).

The fish face of a woman stared back at her. ¡San Onofre, protégeme!

It must be the Jehovahs. They always came in pairs, so the other one must be hiding somewhere. She knew their tricks! She didn't want to talk to them anymore; last time she let them in they left a *Watchtower* with the headline DO THE DEAD KNOW WHAT THE LIVING ARE DOING?

She stealthily brought her eye back up to the peephole and observed the woman cross the street and disappear down Vigil Lane. Very strange: the Jehovahs always worked one side of the street at a time. And this one was by herself!

Though it was getting light now, doña Eulalia did not dare yet open the curtains, for fear the woman would notice if and when she came back up the lane. She kept her eye at the peephole, but the woman did not come back. In another minute, the sun exploded over the mountain, blinding her.

She sat on the banco in the parlor and watched the circular rainbow from the peephole tremble above the hearth. It was a lovely thing, that quivering rainbow, but it didn't answer the troubling question: who was the messenger at the door?

The widower don Raimundo had awoken that morning to find his telephone dead, and had sent his new housekeeper, Mrs. Apodaca, to the Baca house up the road to report the problem to the telephone company from their phone. But when she returned, she told don Raimundo that no one had answered the door.

"But that's impossible!" he said. "They have a house full of chamacos who must be getting ready for school!"

Mrs. Apodaca shrugged. "I heard no children, just the silence of the tomb."

Don Raimundo stared at her. "Which house did you go to?"

"The first on the left, like you said."

"¡San Blas, ayúdame! I said the house on the right! The Baca family!"

"No, don Raimundo. You said left."

"La gran . . . So now what?"

"So now nothing. I'll go back to the house on the right. Though I'm sure you told me the one on the left, don Raimundo."

"No, wait. Never mind. Maybe the apparatus will fix itself."

Mrs. Apodaca picked up the receiver, heard no dial tone, shrugged, and went back to her sweeping.

Doña Eulalia thought about the slightly hunched back of the woman who had rung her doorbell and then disappeared down the road. Where had she seen that back before? Yes — hunkered over a broom, sweeping don Raimundo's portal! That was his new housekeeper!

Now she was worried. What had don Raimundo's housekeeper wanted? It had been years since she had anything to do with Raimundo. How many years? Fifty-one! That long since she had said anything more than "adios" when they passed.

The "adioses" she said to him were different from those she said to others. Usually she said "adio-os" like that, extending the *o* indulgently and smiling. But with Raimundo it had always been rapid and breathless. Anything more and her husband might have spied it. It was not for nothing that her husband was called El Gavilán Tuerto, the one-eyed hawk; he spent his days noiselessly cruising the roads above the village in his rusted El Camino, and claimed he could read lips at a distance of fifty rods. Even now, half a year after her husband's death, doña Eulalia and don Raimundo still seemed afraid to speak to each other, as if El Gavilán still had his eye on them, de ultratumba.

But now Raimundo was trying to communicate with her. She wondered what it could be all about. She gazed at the trembling rainbow above the hearth, which was like the eye of some miraculous or terrible bird, and trembled with it.

Don Raimundo watched the first morning light illuminate the telephone wires bright as train rails before it touched the apple blossoms in his ancient orchard. As always in the morning, he marveled at that pure light, and marveled at how such pure and delicate flowers could burst from things as old and gnarled as those trees. Some kind of miracle.

A tall lilac hedge, heavy with blooms, bordered the orchard. At either end of the lilacs stood a Russian olive, also full of flowers and crazy with bees. Last fall, shortly after El Gavilán died, don Raimundo had slaughtered his chickens from a wire strung from the branches of those two olives, and he believed it was their blood that had made the hedge so thick this year. Behind the hedge, hidden from view, was a little hueco, a low place filled with cottonwood cotton, which had made a bed for him and Eulalia another spring fifty-one years ago, not forgotten.

But now don Raimundo was as worried about doña Eulalia as she was about him. Why hadn't she answered her door when Mrs. Apodaca had knocked on it? After all, she was a notoriously early riser; that's why her friends called her "la comadre madrugona." Why wasn't she answering? The silence of a tomb, Mrs. Apodaca said!

Something bad had happened to Raimundo, doña Eulalia was sure of it. Only that could account for the unexpected appearance of his housekeeper at her door. Don Raimundo was on his deathbed, perhaps, and from his deathbed he had called for her. She could not refuse such a summons. It would be the last time she would see him, the last time she would look into those deep jet eyes, which she hadn't looked into for fifty-one years and which were perhaps now growing milky with death . . .

Because what was certain was that she would not be going to his funeral. Why give the bad tongues more cizaña fodder to chew on? She had too much vergüenza to put up with that.

And it was that same vergüenza, that sense of honor and dignity, that kept her from rushing over right now. No; call first. If he answered, it meant he wasn't deathly sick, and she would just hang up. If the housekeeper answered, she'd simply ask her what she had wanted. She looked up the number and dialed. Busy. She waited and tried again. Busy. The housekeeper must be calling somebody! A doctor, no doubt, an ambulance!

Don Raimundo had often thought about how much he esteemed his telephone, that apparatus others took so much for granted. And often he had thought how much easier things would have been between him and Eulalia had they each had a telephone years ago. El Gavilán may have had a sharp eye and tremendous suspicion, but he was, for all that, thick as cork; how easily he, Raimundo, and Eulalia could have arranged meetings over the phone! But by the time they both had the machines — the Martínezes didn't get theirs until 1970 — it seemed too late to start things again. Too much water under the bridge, too many decades of her furtive adioses. Too late to be nineteen again.

These days he used it frequently for things others scorned and deemed useless, such as the Time and Weather Service. That was what he had been trying to call this morning when he discovered the line was dead. Yesterday, a completely clear day like today, the service's strange computer voice had said "snow." This morning, for amusement, he had wanted to see if it was still saying snow. He knew better: the lone starling sitting on the telephone wire singing its song like dripping water announced thawing, not freezing. The bad weather was finished for this year, and the apples and apricots were going to set well. It was going to be a good year.

But that blank sound, that no sound, from the phone had not been a good omen. Why would it malfunction on such a clear and promising day? That was why he had sent Mrs. Apodaca so immediately to the Baca house (he was sure he had said the house to the right!) to report the problem to the telephone company. And then she had come back to report a silence from Eulalia's, a silence as dead as that from the phone!

Something was de a tiro wrong. He had to call her. If she would not answer the door, perhaps at least she would be able to reach the phone. He grabbed the skinny telephone book and thrust it at Mrs. Apodaca.

"Your eyes are better than mine! Look up her number! Martínez, what was her husband's real name? Epifanio! Epifanio Martínez, look it up! We've got to call! She must be in danger."

Mrs. Apodaca blinked at him. "But the phone's broken, don Raimundo!"

"Oh, of course. Qué bruto. That's the whole problem, ¿que no?"

"That's only part of it," said Mrs. Apodaca, laughing. "The other is that you have a fever in the brain!"

Doña Eulalia was in a hurry to see about Raimundo, but not so much that she did not take the time to fix her hair and put on chile-red lipstick from a stick so old and dry it was almost chalk. But she stayed deliciously naked beneath her bathrobe, and when she stepped outside she felt the crisp and perfumed May breeze voluptuous on her skin. She started down dusty Vigil Lane, and stopped. The scent from the lilacs and Russian olives bordering his huerto was irresistible. . . . Looking around to see that no one was watching, she slipped through the living fence and into the orchard.

"Fever or no," Raimundo declared, "I'm going to look over the orchard." He intended to cut through the orchard straight to Eulalia's back door, but he couldn't have said why he chose this route, or why he couldn't tell Mrs. Apodaca where he was really going.

"Put on your boots, then," Mrs. Apodaca ordered.

He stepped over the border of iris, translucent purple petals like stained glass, and made his way to the lilacs. As he neared the hueco of his and Eulalia's dalliance fifty-one years ago, that gentle depression soon to be full again of fresh cottonwood cotton, he heard the crunch of footsteps on last year's fallen leaves.

"¿Quién vive?"

"¡Gente de paz!"

When he stepped into view, her hand flew to her mouth. "¡María santísima!"

"¡Qué milagro!"

"Eres tú . . ."

"Y tú . . ."

And it was indeed a sort of miracle, because when he got back home, having shaken the white petals from his hair and brushed off his trousers, Mrs. Apodaca, with a sly look on her face, handed him the phone: it worked. He dialed, and Eulalia, having just brushed herself off too, answered.